De

Part 1: The Shadow

©Alice Jamison

This document is geared towards providing exact and reliable information in regards to the topic and issue covered. The publication is sold with the idea that the publisher is not required to render accounting, officially permitted, or otherwise, qualified services. If advice is necessary, legal or professional, a practiced individual in the profession should be ordered.

Also by Alice Jamison

Agony, Ecstasy & Crime
Agony, Ecstasy & Crime Fatal Vows
Agony, Ecstasy & Crime You Are My Drug
Agony, Ecstasy & Crime Disappeared Book 3

Bloodlust
Bloodlust Disturbing the Peace
Bloodlust A New Thirst Book

Cool Blue
Cool Blue After Midnight A Bad Boy Romance
Cool Blue Molten Gold A Bad Boy Romance
Cool Blue Passion Red A Bad Boy Romance
Cool Blue Midnight Black A Bad Boy Romance

Deadly Secrets
Deadly Secrets The Shadow (Billionaire Shape-Shifter Romance Series Book 1)

Deadly Secrets Secrets Revealed (Billionaire Shape-Shifter Romance Series Book 2)
Deadly Secrets The Fight for Love (Billionaire Shape-Shifter Romance Series Book 3)
Deadly Secrets Free (Billionaire Shape-Shifter Romance Series Book 4)
Deadly Secrets Threats (Billionaire Shape-Shifter Romance Series Book 5)
Deadly Secrets Torn Apart (Billionaire Shape-Shifter Romance Series Book 6)
Deadly Secrets Escape (Billionaire Shape-Shifter Romance Series Book 7)
Deadly Secrets Peace (Billionaire Shape-Shifter Romance Series Book 8)

Enchanted Souls Series
Enchanted Souls Series Moonlight
Enchanted Souls Series Tour book 2
Enchanted Souls Series The Secret Of The Glow Book 3
Enchanted Souls Series Return To Crested Valley Book 4
Enchanted Souls Series Forever Book 5

Passion Lust And Fire
Passion Lust And Fire Claim Me Like There's No Tomorrow Book 1
If I Can't Have You No One Can
Passion Lust And Fire Whispers Of The Night Book 3

Seducing The Billionaire

Seducing The Billionaire The Barista And The Billionaire Book 1
A Prince's Betrayal The Barista And The Billionaire Book 2
Chaos of Past Secrets The Barista And The Billionaire Book 3
Engaged in a Whirlwind Weekend The Barista And The Billionaire Book 4
The Final Encounter The Barista And The Billionaire

The Penthouse
The Penthouse (The Meeting Part Two)
The Penthouse (The Rules Part Three)
The Penthouse The Offer Part Four
The Penthouse Part One

Wolf Quest
Wolf Quest: Temptation of the Wolf
Wolf Quest: Passion Of The Wolf Book 2
Wolf Quest: Pleasure Of The Wolf Book 3

World's End
World's End Apocalypse Drake Book 1
World's End: Artificial Drake Book 2
World's End: Wings Of Drake Book 3

Standalone
Vampire Magic
Her Secret Tiger

Deadly Secrets Box Set Volumes 1 - 3 Billionaire Shape-Shifter Romance Series

Enchanted Souls Series Bundle (Books 1 - 3)

Gentle Push

Kill Me Gently With Passion

Cool Blue A Bad Boy Romance 1 - 4 Bundle

Gentle Push, Her Secret Tiger, Kill Me Gently With Passion 3 Book Bundle

World's End 3 Book Bundle

Mithir and Verona The Dragon's Surrender

A Secret Shade Of Mysterious Bear Shifters

This World Is Full Of Men

He's Watching Me

I'll Always Have Your Back (A Bad Boy Billionaire Romance)

A Mysterious Bad Boy

Spice

I Thought You Were the One

Get out of my Life

The Penthouse The Call Part 5

Wolf Quest: 3 Book Bundle

A Billionaire Romance Series Bundle Books 1 - 5 The Penthouse 7 Erotica Bundle Stories Hot Stories Of Sex, BDSM, Domination And Submission That Will Make You Wet!

Chapter One

Elsa Grey ran down the long passageway as she looked back in terror. Panic rose up; threatening to suffocate her. She was being pursued by an unknown entity. She stopped to peer into the darkness. Her eyes widened as her vision slowly adjusted. Her pursuer was nowhere to be seen. She swallowed hard; the sound audible in the silence. Maybe it's gone, she thought as relief slowly started to set in. Suddenly, yellow eyes flashed before her and sharp claws reached out to grab her.

Elsa woke with a start and abruptly sat up in bed. Her body was washed in cold sweat and her breaths came out in ragged puffs. The sheets were in a tangled pile around her waist; some spilling onto the floor. Her eyes roamed around her small apartment. She sighed in relief. It's just a nightmare. Combing her fingers through her hair, she plopped back down on her back and stared up at the ceiling. Recently, she had been having the same terrifying dream almost every night. What was going on? She avoided horror movies - it did not stem from something she had seen. She definitely had not read anything about shadows or creatures with yellow eyes either. She sighed into the silence of the room. I am way too stressed. Elsa closed her eyes and relaxed and soon fell back into a deep sleep.

Elsa rolled out of the bed reluctantly at the sound of her alarm clock the following morning. It was time for her to get ready for work and she felt terrible. She had had another nightmare after she had fallen back asleep; and it had taken her a long while to fall asleep again. She studied her reflection in the bathroom mirror; dark circles beneath her eyes marred her creamy skin, her dark brown eyes were bloodshot and her shoulder length auburn hair hung in a messy curtain around her face. I look like something out of a horror movie. She turned away from her unappealing image and stepped into the bathtub.

She dressed quickly; putting on a pair of flared cut grey trousers and a purple silk button down blouse. She slipped her small feet into purple pumps and arranged her hair in an elegant chignon. Putting on minimal makeup, she stood back and studied her professional but stylish appearance with satisfaction.

Elsa grabbed her handbag and headed out the door. The humidity of Georgia's summer air hit her as she stepped out of her apartment building. It was only eight thirty in the morning but the sun already glared at her with harsh intensity. Elsa looked around her neighborhood as she walked to the bus stop. It wasn't the safest or the nicest, but it was what she could afford. She had graduated from college one year prior and had almost immediately landed a job as a data entry clerk at a pharmaceutical company. It wasn't the most glamorous or exciting job, but it paid the bills. She had had no money whatsoever and had eagerly taken the job. She had worked to pay her own way through school. It had been a struggle, but she had done it.

A pang of sadness hit Elsa as she reflected on her lonely childhood. Both of her parents had been killed in a car accident when she was just nine years old, leaving her with only one surviving relative; her old, miserable paternal uncle who had not had the slightest idea of how to raise a child. Henry Grey was a very wealthy man, who did not relate well to other people, especially children. Elsa was raised in a cold, loveless environment. She was shown no affection by her uncle. He ignored her, ensuring only that she had the necessary things which were food, shelter and education. She supposed she should be grateful for that much. When she had graduated high school, Henry made no offer to lend financial assistance for college and Elsa had not asked. She had been happy to get the opportunity to move out of the old, creepy mansion she had grown up in.

Elsa had packed her bags and set out to make life on her own. She had not seen her uncle in five years. They had not even spoken over the phone. Elsa had tried calling a few times after she had left but she was always ignored, so she had stopped trying. It was obvious that her uncle did not want to hear from her.

A bus finally pulled up in front of her; bringing her back to the present. The door opened and she stepped onto the bus and took a seat at the front. The bus made its way through the sprawling city of Atlanta. Elsa stared out the window, admiring her surroundings. She was glad she had left her uncle's home in Pennsylvania. She preferred the warmth of Georgia and she had wanted to get as far away as possible from the state where her parents had died and where she was treated with cold disdain for most of her childhood. She had seen Georgia State University on a brochure shortly before graduating high school and had randomly applied. She had chosen to remain in the state after graduating.

The bus came to a stop and Elsa got off. She stood in front of the huge building in which she worked and took a deep breath. It was another day of working alongside people she could not seem to connect with. *Why do I have to be so terrible at making friends?* She was always surrounded by so many people, yet, she always felt so alone. Her shoulders drooped slightly as she walked up the steps to the entrance.

"Good morning, Elsa," came a cheerful voice as she walked into the office. She turned around to see Lisa, her co-worker, smiling broadly at her. Lisa Taylor worked in the neighboring cubicle and she always made an effort to have conversations with Elsa. Elsa always admired Lisa's perfect brown skin and edgy pixie haircut. She often wondered what Lisa was doing in an office cubicle and not on a runway. She also admired how kind Lisa was to her despite her lack of social skills.

"Good morning," Elsa replied.

"You look nice as usual."

Elsa glanced down at her attire and blushed. She always made the effort to look her best. She wasn't very sociable and she didn't have much money; but at least no one could say she had a terrible sense of fashion. She took pride in her appearance - apparently it was the only thing she had going for her. She threw Lisa a shy smile, "Thanks," She sat down in her cubicle and prepared herself to begin working.

Lisa stuck her head around the thin partition, "Hey, don't look now, but Jonathan is heading this way."

Fighting the temptation, Elsa kept herself from looking back. Jonathan was their supervisor and many of the women in the office had lusted after the tall, handsome, blond haired man. Elsa didn't see what was so special about him. But then again, she was completely flawed when it came to interacting with human beings. So, what did she know?

"Oh my God, he's stopping right here," Lisa whispered excitedly.

Elsa looked up at the figure that loomed over her. Jonathan was smiling brightly, "Hi Elsa, how are you?"

"Uh, I'm fine, thanks," Elsa responded hesitantly and turned back to her computer. Why is he always stopping to talk to me? She did not appreciate his constant personal greetings or the other women in the office's seething looks every time he stopped to speak with her.

Jonathan stood for a few moments, studying the back of Elsa's head with a combination of confusion and amazement. "Okay great, catch you later!" he said and walked off.

Lisa pushed her chair partly into Elsa's cubicle. "I'm just going to come right out and say it, you are totally clueless."

Elsa threw her a confused look, "What do you mean?"

"It is obvious to the world that Jonathan likes you, but you don't even seem to realize."

Elsa stared at her blankly. It came as a shock to her that Lisa would even think that Jonathan was interested in her. "Well, if he is, I am certainly not interested. He is not my type."

Lisa's brows rose in surprise, she moved closer to Elsa, her attention now fully captivated. She hadn't heard Elsa utter a word about her personal life. "Is that so? What is your type?"

Elsa slightly panicked. She didn't expect Lisa to take the subject any further. She didn't know her type; in all her twenty-three years, she had never even had a boyfriend. "Uh, well I-I"

"Get back to work ladies," Jonathan said sternly as he walked passed again.

Thank God. Elsa breathed a sigh of relief. She had dodged that bullet. She could not take the humiliation of letting Lisa in on the fact that she didn't know the first thing about men. Lisa swung her head around the partition, "We will continue our conversation over lunch." She continued before Elsa could refuse, "That's right you and me, lunch, later. I'm not taking no for an answer. You're going off for vacation soon and I won't see you for two weeks."Lisa quickly disappeared back into her cubicle.

Elsa groaned inwardly, she was not anticipating lunch with Lisa. But, she supposed she should make the effort to be friendly with her co-worker. After all, Lisa was the only person at work with whom she exchanged more than one sentence at a time. She made up her mind, before she went on vacation the following week, she was going to make one friend. She wasn't sure if she should call Lisa a friend yet, because she wasn't very good with the dynamics of relationships, but it seemed promising. Elsa resigned herself to work.

Three and a half hours later, Elsa pushed her chair back; glad to finally be able to take her eyes off of her computer screen. Her eyes hurt and her fingers were numb from hours of typing. "Are you ready?" Lisa asked cheerfully.

Elsa nodded; "Sure," she collected her handbag and followed Lisa to the door. Exiting the building, they walked to a nearby bistro. The casual ambiance and the lack of a crowd helped to put Elsa at ease. She was a little nervous about spending an entire hour talking with someone. Once they were seated, a waitress immediately approached them. They quickly placed their orders and settled in.

Lisa studied Elsa, making her even more nervous. She finally broke the silence, "We have worked together for almost a year now, and we have never had lunch together. That is unacceptable."

"I guess," Elsa replied softly.

Lisa smiled, relax Elsa. I know you're not very talkative, so I will do most of the talking, like I usually do; everyone knows I have a big mouth." She let out a girlish giggle that made Elsa laugh. She relaxed instantly; maybe lunch with her co-worker wasn't going to be so bad after all. "Can I ask you something Elsa?"

Elsa glanced at Lisa, a little afraid of what she would come out with. "Um, ok."

"How come I never see you interact with anyone? Well, except me; and I practically have to force words out of you. Please don't take any offense, I'm just curious. I mean, you're such a nice woman."

Elsa gawked at her; Lisa thought she was nice. That must mean that she actually likes me. That assumption helped her to open up. "Well, I don't have great people skills. I usually feel awkward around people so I keep to myself - I always have. You are the first person I have ever sat across from like this and actually...talked to."

"Well, I guess we should do this more often then, and work on those people skills," Lisa said, winking.

Elsa gaped at the woman before her, surprised that she did not judge her or say she was 'stuck up' like most people did. Elsa smiled brightly; maybe this was a sign that she wouldn't be lonely for the rest of her life. "I would like that," she replied.

Lisa leaned in and whispered conspiratorially, "So, let's get down to business. Do you have a boyfriend? You said you weren't interested in Jonathan."

Elsa nearly groaned out loud. She had hoped Lisa would forget all about that subject. "I don't have a boyfriend."

Lisa gasped, dramatically clutching her chest, "No way, you are way too gorgeous not to have a significant other."

Shrugging, Elsa stated, "I don't even know how to talk to men, so I just ignore them."

"You poor thing," Lisa said, shaking her head. "But you did say you had a type, so that is a start. Describe your perfect man."

Elsa thought hard. "Well, I guess I want him to be good looking," she stopped, searching for words and Lisa smiled and nodded encouragingly. Elsa thought of the few romance novels she had read. She had always fantasized about meeting a man just like the ones in the novels - one who would sweep her off her feet and take her away from her lonely existence. They would live happily ever after. "I suppose, I want a man straight out of a romance novel; talk, dark, handsome, and charming."

Lisa sighed, "Yes, every girl wants Prince Charming to come and sweep her off her feet."

"Fairytales aren't real, so I guess I will never find the perfect man."

"Nonsense," Lisa scoffed. "I bet if you look hard enough when you go on vacation, you will find your perfect man. What do you have planned by the way?"

"Nothing really," Elsa answered. The women waited in silence as the waitress set their food before them and walked away.

"I have a solution to that problem." Lisa dug around in her handbag, coming up with a colorful brochure. She handed it to Elsa. "I got this from a travel agency a few days ago."

"Caribbean Paradise Cruise: come aboard and experience true paradise," Elsa read. "Enjoy your choice of one of our seven day or fourteen day cruises."

"Doesn't it sound wonderful? I would love to go on a cruise, but my vacation isn't until two more months," Lisa said sadly. "You should go!"

"It sounds lovely and I could do with some relaxation, but I can't afford it." Elsa handed the brochure back to Lisa.

"No, keep it. You never know what could happen."

Elsa shrugged and slipped the brochure into her bag. There was nothing that could possibly happen that would allow her such an opportunity. I am not that lucky, she thought.

That evening, Elsa was seated on a bus, on her way home. She rolled her neck, trying to get some relief from the pain she felt. Hours spent sitting up in a hard chair staring at a computer screen was not good for the joints and muscles. It was torture on her body. She took comfort in the fact that she would get a full two weeks off soon. She was finally in her neighborhood. She stepped off the bus and made the short walk to her apartment building.

Once inside, she dropped her bag on the coffee table and plopped down in the nearest couch. She glanced around her apartment. What a dump, she thought. She smiled inwardly; but it's my dump. She was proud that she had achieved something on her own. The flashing red light on her answering machine caught her attention. She got up to check the message.

"Hello, Elsa Grey. This is Harriot Billings, your Uncle Henry Grey's lawyer. I am relieved that I finally located you. Please give me a call as soon as you get this, message." Elsa stood in shock as the female voice rattled off a phone number. Why would her uncle's lawyer want to talk to her? Confused, she hesitantly dialed the phone number that was left on the machine.

"Hello, this is Harriot Billings."

"Uh, hi this is Elsa Grey."

"Hi Miss Grey, I'm glad you called."

"What is this about?" Elsa asked cautiously.

"I am very sorry to tell you that your uncle has passed away."

Elsa was silent for a few seconds as she processed what Harriot Billings had just told her. She didn't know what she was feeling. She was almost certain that a pang of sadness had run through her. She took a deep breath, "When did he pass?"

"Three days ago, it took me a while to track you down. I found no phone number for you in your uncle's documents. However, your name is on his will. That is why I contacted you."

He put me on his will? "Are you absolutely sure?"

"Of course Miss Grey, you are his only living relative. Is there any way you can come to Pennsylvania?"

"I won't be able to make it up there until next week."

"That will be fine. We can discuss the details further. I'm sorry for your loss, Miss Grey. See you soon."

Elsa hung up the phone. She wasn't sure what to do or how to feel. Uncle Henry was dead, he had been her only relative, and she hadn't found out until three days later. Now she truly was alone in the world. They had not been close, she hadn't even spoken to him in five years, but tears still sprung to her eyes, though they did not spill over. She wished things could have been different between her and her uncle. Maybe she should have made more of an effort to get in touch with him or even gone to visit him in Pennsylvania at least once. She thought he hated her. To find out he had left her something came as a great shock.

Chapter Two

Elsa stood on the front steps of the massive old mansion, where she had spent much of her childhood. It felt strange being back in Northumberland, Pennsylvania. She never considered that she would be back in the state or at the home where she had no happy memories. The house looming before her was hundreds of years old; and it had not been maintained properly. Elsa shuddered, despite the warm mid-July breeze. The house looked creepy; like the perfect setting for a horror movie. She wanted to turn around and leave, but she had agreed to meet with Harriot Billings at her uncle's house. She glanced at her watch. The lawyer should be here any minute now.

She turned around to take in her surroundings. It really was a nice country setting. The house was in the center of a large piece of land - the closest neighbor was at least one mile away. If the house was in good condition and the lawn and the trees were manicured, the place would be beautiful. But it had been depressing and drab the day she had moved in and it remained the same years later. "Miss Grey?"

Elsa turned to see a slender African American woman, sporting an expensive, well tailored suit walking toward her. "Yes, Harriot Billings?"

"That's right," the woman smiled, reaching for her hand. "It's very nice to meet you."

Elsa shook the lawyer's well manicured hand, "Nice to meet you too."

"I hope you had a good trip - you came quite a long way."

"It was okay," Elsa responded. The short flight had been uneventful.

"Thank you for meeting me here. Shall we go inside?" Harriot headed up the steps toward the front door. Elsa followed, watching Harriot fish a single key out of her handbag and unlock the huge double wooden doors. They screeched open, revealing a large, dark, open space. Definitely creepy, Elsa thought. She stepped into the house and looked around the dank, decrepit structure. It smelled as if the place had been locked up for years. Had her uncle really stayed in this health hazard up to his last day? She wouldn't be surprised if he had died from a health issue he had developed because of this house. Harriot turned to her and handed her the key.

Elsa gave her a confused glance; Harriot wave her hand encompassing the poor excuse for a home. "This is all yours," she said.

You cannot be serious! "What do you mean it's mine?" Elsa asked.

"Your uncle left it for you in his will."

"Wow, that's um... great." Elsa wasn't sure how else to respond. She glanced around again. What was she supposed to do with this? "Did my uncle die here?"

"Oh no, he was in a nursing home for the past two years, he could no longer live here on his own."

Elsa was relieved. So, her uncle had not died in this dilapidated house all alone. As much as she resented him for her less than loving upbringing, she would not have wanted that for the miserable old man. She held the key out to Harriot, "Not that I don't appreciate my uncle's generosity, but I really don't need this house."

Harriot shook her head, "the house is yours to do whatever you wish. That includes putting it up for sale if you so desire. There is more to your uncle's will. Let us find a seat and I will tell you the rest."

Oh, there's more. What else could her uncle have left her? She couldn't imagine. They entered the kitchen, to find chairs they could use. Elsa pulled a pack of tissue from her handbag to dust off the chairs and a portion of the long dining table. She eyed the ancient looking chair, wondering if it would support her weight. This entire place is falling apart.

"Ok, let's get down to business," Harriot said, placing her leather briefcase on the table. Elsa watched silently as she opened the case and took out a few pieces sheets of paper. "Along with this estate, your uncle also left you a total of one million dollars."

Elsa's eyebrows shot up. She was astounded! Her uncle had not offered her any financial assistance when she was in college. "Well that was awfully kind of him, one whole million out of all of his millions," Elsa said sarcastically. Harriot threw her a strange look, her eyebrows going skyward. "It's a long story," Elsa muttered. Her uncle's lawyer did not need to know the history of her relationship with her uncle or the resentment she harbored toward him. She wanted to tell Harriot that she didn't want a penny of Henry Grey's money; but she quickly reconsidered. She could use the money to get herself out of her current apartment and find one in a safer neighborhood.

Harriot continued to read, "You get half now and half when you turn twenty-five."

"Ok," Elsa supposed she was grateful to her uncle for the thinking of her; after all the years of pretty much ignoring her existence.

"Well, Miss Grey that is all."

"Thank you very much Ms. Billings," Elsa stood up and shook Harriot's hand.

"Do enjoy the rest of your stay in Pennsylvania, Miss Grey. Take care and I will be in touch."

The stylish lawyer took her leave, leaving Elsa alone in the creepy house. Elsa looked around. Could she spend the night alone in the house? She barely had enough money for a night in a hotel. Suddenly, a noise from an unknown source sounded in the silence. Elsa gasped and rushed to the door. Maybe I can afford one night in a hotel after all. Her flight back to Georgia was tomorrow afternoon; she would spend what little money she had rather than spend the night in her newly inherited house. She quickly locked the door, and walked away from the creepy house. She doubted she would keep it.

Elsa found a cheap hotel to spend the night in. She sat on the linen sheets in silence thinking about her childhood with her uncle. She thought of how much she had craved his love and attention and how she had never got it. She had been devastated when her parents had died and she had hoped Uncle Henry would provide some comfort and reassurance, but it never came. He only treated her with cold gruffness and pretended that she didn't exist. Sadness washed over her at the memory, but also because her uncle was gone and they never got a chance to work on having some kind of family relationship.

Elsa sighed, it was too late now, and she couldn't beat herself up over it any longer. Uncle Henry had actually left her a small portion of his money. It was still incredible to her; five hundred thousand dollars now; and another five hundred thousand dollars in two years. She had never received so much money at once, and she probably never would if she continued with her current job. *I can do a lot with that much money.* Suddenly, she remembered the brochure that Lisa had handed her. She had forgotten all about it. She had thought going on that cruise was only going to happen in her dreams. *Well I must be dreaming now, because it seems I can afford to go after all.* She looked down at her bag beside her and reached inside. She had to shove several things aside before she found the crumpled brochure and smoothed the paper. Elsa beamed as she read over the details again. *Oh yeah, I am so going on this floating paradise!* She clapped her hands in glee and threw herself down on the bed in excitement. She looked up at the ceiling. Now she could really enjoy her vacation! She would call the cruise line first thing tomorrow and be on that ship by Friday, for seven days of paradise. She would be back in time to have two days to get ready for work. It would be perfect.

The following day, Elsa was back in Georgia. She called Lisa to give her the good news. "No way!" Lisa shouted into the phone. "I'm sorry about your uncle, are you alright?"

"Yes, I'm fine. We weren't really that close, but I'm still a little sad about his passing."

"So he left you a mansion and one million dollars? That was kind of him, considering you weren't close."

"It was - it was totally unexpected," Elsa replied.

"I'm so excited for you. You're actually going on that cruise!"

"Yes, I called the cruise line this morning and made the arrangements, I'm leaving for Florida on Thursday and the ship will be leaving port on Friday. I'm excited too! I have never done anything like this before."

Lisa sighed dramatically, "How I wish I could join you! We would have so much fun."

"I wish you were coming with me too. As nice as going on a Caribbean cruise sounds, it's going to be awfully lonely."

"We can plan another trip together - maybe next year."

"That would be awesome." Elsa smiled at the thought of going on vacation with the vivacious Lisa.

"I have to go," Lisa whispered. "The boss is heading this way. We will talk before you leave. Oh and we need to go shopping for your trip." Lisa let out a low, excited squeal before hanging up.

Elsa smiled broadly. She and Lisa had shared lunch together every day before Elsa's vacation leave started. Elsa felt comfortable with Lisa and had opened up more and more each day. Lisa was a genuinely friendly soul and Elsa was drawn to her. She could finally say that she actually had a friend. Going on vacation with Lisa was truly a comforting thought. But, she would be going alone this time around.

On Wednesday evening Elsa met Lisa in town for their shopping expedition. "You know, it is quite a lonely time at work without you there," Lisa stated as they entered one of Elsa's favorite clothing stores. "I habitually stick my head around the wall to say something to you, and you aren't there."

Elsa giggled, picturing Lisa whipping around to her cubicle as excitedly as she usually did. "I'm sorry, I will be back soon." They browsed the various aisles, picking out articles of clothing worthy of a Caribbean cruise.

"You need to look spectacular, Elsa. You could very well find the man of your dreams on this vacation."

Elsa threw Lisa a doubtful glance, "Probably not, and even if I did, I wouldn't have the slightest idea of how to talk to him. So, he would probably think I was a weirdo and run away."

"Oh please, have you looked in the mirror lately? You don't even have to say a word to get a man. Just stand there and be your gorgeous self."

Elsa still wasn't convinced. The only hope she had about her vacation was to get away from her lonely, humdrum life for at least a week. Maybe she would finally get a good night's rest on the cruise ship. She hadn't been able to sleep through the night in weeks; she was constantly awakened by her strange dreams. She couldn't figure out what the dreams were about, where they stemmed from or why she was having them. *Maybe I need to see a psychiatrist.* She hadn't shared her nightly dreams with Lisa, for fear that her new found friend would think she was crazy.

At the end of their shopping trip, Lisa and Elsa prepared to part ways. "I'm going to miss you Elsa," Lisa said.

"I'm going to miss you too, "Elsa replied. "I will be able to send you e-mails though. I read on the brochure that there is an internet café on board that is open twenty four hours a day."

"Awesome, so you can update me daily about your time on board and I can live vicariously through you for the entire seven days." Lisa laughed and Elsa couldn't help but join in.

"Yes I will e-mail you everyday, it will be like you are on vacation with me!"

"Great, so you take care of yourself and stay safe. I can't wait for you to get back."

Elsa leaned into Lisa's embrace, "I will."

Back at her apartment, Elsa busied herself packing for her trip. She glanced around her apartment. When she got back, she would search for a much better living space.

Chapter Three

Wow, this is beautiful, Elsa thought as she stood staring up at the large ship. The white vessel had the words Caribbean Paradise sprawled across it in bold red letters. The ship was about six decks tall. She had done some research the night before; The Caribbean Paradise was a smaller cruise line which held about two thousand and five hundred passengers. She preferred the smaller ship with less passengers; she hated crowds. Two thousand five hundred people is still quite a lot.

She made her way to the elevated ramp to follow the group of people boarding the ship. Elsa glanced around at the many people around her; there was a variety of different characters, ranging from young to old. There were couples and families with children. Her cheeks flamed. Was she the only single person on the cruise? She groaned inwardly, how embarrassing. She prayed that the line would hurry and move along, so that she could go and hide in her cabin. Was it her imagination, or was she getting strange looks from the other passengers? Maybe going on this cruise by herself wasn't such a great idea after all. She shook her head, she had to be imagining things; no one probably even noticed her. She squared her shoulders and proceeded on board. She handed a crew member her key card and checked in. Entering the main atrium of the ship, she joined the group gathering on the main deck. She was told that the cabins were not ready yet and she would have to wait in the public area for a while.

Elsa looked around; she felt out of place standing alone while other people chatted excitedly and laughed. She hurriedly moved away from the crowd to peer over the railing in to the crystal blue water. Great, this is how it's going to be the entire time I'm here; me standing alone staring into the water. She prayed for her cabin to be ready soon, so she could go in there and hide. She shook her head; no she couldn't hide in her cabin like a hermit for the entire cruise. She had to at least attempt to interact with the other passengers. Maybe someone will see me hanging around by myself and take pity on me, she thought. Or, maybe by some miracle she would find the man of her dreams like Lisa had said. Elsa snorted; yeah right, like that's going to happen.

Someone brushed against her and brought her out of her deep thoughts. She whipped around to see who it was. A tall willowy man was staring at her intently, with hooded eyes. Despite the warmth of the summer weather, a chill ran down Elsa's spine. She quickly turned and scurried away from the ominous looking man. Well, he looks creepy. She wondered if the cruise line did background checks on their passengers. The man she had just encountered gave her a bad feeling in the pit of her stomach. Why had he stared at her like that? How impolite! She couldn't help but shudder at the memory of his piercing blue eyes. Still thinking about the strange man, Elsa was not paying attention to where she was going. "Oomph ouch," she suddenly collided with a large, hard body. "Oh my God, I'm so sorry, I-I wasn't looking where I was going," she stuttered, as strong hands reached out to steady her.

"It's quite alright, no harm done," said an unknown voice.

Elsa shuddered, this time out of sexual awareness, rather than a bad feeling. The British accented, deep baritone voice slid over her entire body like a soft caress, and the hands that were still on her arms caused shock waves to course through her. Oh my. Her eyes slowly ascended, passing over a wide chest and toned biceps; finally landing on a beautiful male face. Oh my. The man had a medium-light skin tone as if he spent time in the sun; with deep set green eyes, an aristocratic nose, and a strong square jaw line. His thick black wavy hair brushed his shoulders. His features screamed alpha male. Her knees felt weak, and she prayed she wouldn't embarrass herself by toppling over. His full pink lips curved into a slight smile and Elsa stared up at him wide eyed in wonder. She realized how foolish she must look and shook herself out of her lust induced trance.

"That was entirely my fault, I apologize again," she said softly, trying to avoid his eyes, so as not to be hypnotized by his green gaze.

"It's ok," he said gazing at her with an unidentified expression. "Just try to be more careful." He let go of her arm abruptly and quickly walked away.

Elsa stared after him, confused and absolutely horrified. Oh no, I scared the poor man away with my staring, he must think I'm such an idiot. She mentally kicked herself in the behind. It seemed like he couldn't get away from her fast enough. Elsa hung her head and groaned out loud, ignoring the curious looks from a few other passengers.

Charles looked back at the strange woman who had just bumped into him. He swallowed hard, what was that feeling that had coursed through his body when he touched her? When he had looked into her brown eyes, something inside him had stirred. He had to get away from her fast. He walked quickly, getting as far away from her as possible. He couldn't afford to get involved with anyone. When are the damn cabins going to be ready? He had to get away from all these people; he hated crowds.

He anticipated locking himself away in the expensive suite. The money wasn't the issue; he could more than afford it. He had made billions with his business ventures and wise investments. The fact that he had paid so much money for the cabin and had to wait for hours before being able to occupy it was what really annoyed him. He reached the front of the cruise ship and chose an area away from the crowd. He was glad he could no longer see the red headed woman, who had stirred up unknown feelings inside of him. He ignored the lustful and flirtatious glances women threw his way. He shook his head, weren't these women here with their husbands or significant others? His mind drifted back to the pretty redhead; he wondered if she was on the cruise with a companion. More than likely she was. He shook her from his thoughts immediately.

The Captain finally came on the speakers to announce the ship's departure from the Miami port. Charles glanced at his watch; it was now six thirty in the evening. "It's about time," he muttered to himself.

Hours later, after dinner in one of the restaurants on board, Elsa was finally directed to her cabin. She made her way down to one of the lower decks. She had deliberately chosen a cabin away from the hustle and bustle of the ship's daily activities. She used her key card to unlock the door. The space was like a hotel room, but much smaller. There was a single bed in the center of a room with a wooden desk across from it. To the left of the bed was a comfortable looking butter yellow couch. Elsa looked up to see a large screen television perched on the wall. That closed door must be where the bathroom is. She walked over to the door and pulled it open, she was right.

Elsa exited the bathroom and headed to a set of sliding doors which led to a small balcony with a spectacular view of the ocean. "This is incredible!" she squealed in delight. Her cabin was perfect. It was stylish and cozy. She had splurged a bit when selecting her package. She had thought she might as well make good use of some of her inherited cash to have the best possible vacation. Who knew when she would have this opportunity again? Her bags had arrived at her cabin before her; they were situated on the floor beside the bed. She decided to unpack.

A little while later, Elsa left her cabin. She had to locate the ship's internet café so that she could e-mail Lisa as promised. She followed the confusing directory for about twenty minutes before finally locating the room. She sighed in relief. Finally. She quickly typed Lisa a message.

Dear Lisa,

The ship set sail not too long ago. The trip is okay so far, I'm just a bit lonely. I wish you were here - at least I would have someone to talk to. We will be stopping in the Bahamas in three days. I look forward to that! I've always wanted to go to a Caribbean island.

I met a guy this afternoon, or rather, I nearly knocked him over. He is the most gorgeous man I have ever seen. He is definitely my dream man. I actually talked to him... well sort of. Anyway, I think I have scared him off, so that's the end of that. So far, there is nothing more exciting to tell. I will e-mail again soon.

Elsa

She quickly sent the message off. She wished there was more to tell, but her vacation had been uneventful so far. Elsa left the café and headed back to her cabin. There wasn't much else for her to do at the moment. She was definitely not going solo to the casino or any of the other functions taking place above. She was not that brave. She would take a nice hot shower back at her cabin, snuggle up in bed and watch TV. Yes, that sounds like a good plan. Maybe when she became more accustomed to her environment, she would be bold enough to venture out and experience a little bit of the nightlife on board.

As she strolled down the long passage way toward her cabin, the strange chill she had experience earlier struck her again. It was the same feeling she had experienced when she had looked into the creepy man's eyes. She rubbed her arms to warm herself, and looked back. There was no one there; but she got the strange feeling that she was being watched. She took a deep breath and shook off the feeling. It was just probably just her mind playing tricks on her. There were about two thousand people on the ship; of course it was possible that someone's eyes were on her, out of her private cabin. Despite these reassurances, she increased her pace, almost running to her cabin. She quickly locked the door behind her and let out a sigh. *I have to take my active imagination down a notch.*

After her shower, Elsa relaxed in bed. She flipped through the channels and finally landed on a comedy. She put down the remote and burrowed deeper into the luxurious, fresh smelling sheets. *Hmm, this is nice.* It was so much nicer than her bed back at home. *A girl can get* used to this. Elsa watched the movie until her eyes began to droop. She finally gave in and let sleep consume her.

She found herself running down a dark passageway again, this time it was on the ship. She could barely see through the darkness. What happened to the lights? A sense of urgency pressed on her - she couldn't see it, but she was sure that the shadowy figure pursuing her was near. She had to get away. Who was it? She had not been able to see who it was; or what it was. She could have sworn she had seen claws and yellow eyes. But that was ridiculous; no animals were on the ship. She ran faster, breathing hard. It seemed she had been running for hours. Where was everyone? Why was there no one here to help her? She had boarded the ship with thousands of people, yet there was no one. What is going on?

She reached the back end of the ship; there was nowhere to go except over the rail and into the water. She peered down into to the ocean; it was a raging black abyss. She couldn't jump overboard; she couldn't swim for Christ's sake! There was nowhere left to run. She stood, paralyzed by terror, as the shadow rushed toward her. She let out a piercing scream.

Elsa awoke screaming and thrashing in her bed. She sat up, looking around her. Where was she? Then it all came back to her; she wasn't in her own apartment, she was in a cabin on a cruise ship. She released rapid, shallow breaths. Damn it. her recurring nightmare had followed her on her vacation. She had thought it had been stress related. She wasn't very happy with her life and wanted to get away from it. She had even thought that the shadow in her dream was a metaphor for her life and that she was running, trying to escape it. But she was on a relaxing vacation, in a completely different environment and she was still having the dream. But, this time it was more vivid and more terrifying. At least before, her only choice of escape wasn't to jump to her death in a vast black ocean.

Elsa ran a hand over her face. She had to find some way to get rid of her plaguing nightmare. It was hindering her from getting enough sleep. Glancing at the clock, she sighed and scooted out of bed. It was two o'clock in the morning and she needed to take a walk; maybe after she would be able to fall back asleep. She pulled on a pair of shorts and a t-shirt and headed out the door. As she made her way to the elevator, she stopped. After the dream she'd had, maybe it wasn't the best idea to go walking alone. She started to turn back but shook her head and snorted. She was being ridiculous; it had only been a dream. Obscured figures with yellow eyes and claws were not real; so there was no reason for her to be afraid. She proceeded to the elevator.

Charles had been sleeping, dreaming about the red headed woman with the innocent brown eyes. He had found her alone on the main deck. No one else was in sight. He walked up to her, not saying a word. He held her brown gaze, discovering desire in its depths. She parted her lips invitingly and he couldn't resist. He bent his head and captured her soft lips in his own.

He was abruptly awakened by a scream, coming from below. He jumped up, cocking his head to the side, using his acute hearing to listen. The screaming stopped. His eyes flashed yellow in the darkness. The scream he had heard must have come from one of the cabins below him. Maybe it was someone fooling around. But the need to make sure no one was in actual danger was like a compulsion. He had detected a menacing presence on board earlier.

Could it be the person he had been tracking for months? He had tracked his enemy to this very ship, but then it seemed like he had disappeared into thin air. After the ship had set sail, it crossed Charles' mind that perhaps he had boarded this ship for nothing? Why would his nemesis board a cruise ship? It made no sense for him to put himself in this restricted environment where he could easily be discovered. Charles hopped out of bed and threw on a shirt.

He opened his cabin door and peeped down the passageway. It was empty. He stepped out using his enhanced senses to detect anything out of the ordinary. He made his way to an elevator. He had to check the deck below to see if anything was amiss. The scream he had heard was a sound of terror. He walked through the hallway on the lower deck, noticing nothing out of the ordinary. As he walked further, he caught a whiff of a familiar scent. It was her.

It was the woman who had bumped into him on the main deck. She must occupy one of the cabins nearby. He heard a slight movement and moved swiftly into a dark corner to conceal himself. He peeked around to see a cabin door open, and the woman in his recent dream stepped out. She locked her door and headed for the elevator. Where the hell is she going at this time of night? He thought, annoyed. If the person he thought was on this ship was there, it wasn't safe for her to be walking around by herself at this hour. He waited until the elevator door closed before stepping out of the shadows.

He gave a low growl. He didn't know why he was so concerned about a woman he didn't even know. He tried to convince himself that it was the young innocence that he had detected in her eyes when he had looked down at her. Deep down, he knew it was because of the almost magnetic pull he had felt toward her. But he didn't want to dwell on that fact. Now was not the time for him to get involved with some innocent young girl.

Charles followed the mystery woman's scent all the way to the main deck. He remained in the shadows, watching her as she strolled slowly to the ship's rail to look over into the ocean. Her hair whipped around her, stirred by the cool breeze; her small frame stood unmoving as she stood peering out into the distance. She seemed almost ethereal.

His head whipped around as he sensed someone else approaching. He quickly stepped out of his dark hiding place and sauntered toward the woman. He had to approach her so as to deter anyone with ulterior motives who may come and find her standing alone.

Chapter Four

The hair stood up on the back of Elsa's neck. She wasn't alone on the deck after all. She could feel someone approaching her. She turned to see who it was. Oh my God, it's him. She stood frozen in place as he approached her.

"Couldn't sleep?" He asked softly, sending her a warm smile.

"U-uh no," Elsa stuttered. She gulped, not sure what to do. His close proximity was wreaking pure havoc on her senses. They were the only ones on the deck and he was standing right in front of her. She had no choice to but engage him in conversation. She took a deep steadying breath. You can do this; just pretend you're talking to Lisa. Elsa nearly let out a groan; she couldn't just pretend it was Lisa, for Christ's sake. Lisa wasn't a tall, sexy man with gorgeous green eyes; and she wasn't sexually attracted to Lisa either.

"Me neither," he admitted.

Elsa swallowed nervously and replied "I figured taking a walk would be relaxing."

"Hmm, maybe it wasn't a good idea to come out at this time by yourself."

She laughed nervously, "Well, how dangerous can a cruise ship called Caribbean Paradise be, right?"

He cocked an eyebrow, you have no idea. "You would be surprised. Why didn't you ask your companion to follow you?"

Elsa frowned, "My companion? I'm actually here alone." Her cheeks flamed with humiliation at having to admit that she wasn't on the cruise with a husband or boyfriend. He must think she was a total loser.

"Your significant other must be crazy to allow you to come on this cruise alone."

"I-I don't have a significant other," she gave another nervous giggle "I'm free, single and disengaged."

Charles was surprised by how pleased he was with that information. He joined her, leaning against the rail. "All the men must be blind, where you're from. Where are you from by the way?"

"Georgia," she responded.

"What is your name, woman from Georgia?"

She smiled, "Elsa Grey, and you are?"

He held his hand out, "Charles Grimm the third." She placed her hand in his and shook lightly. He quickly realized that he held on to her delicate hand a few seconds too long, and released it. "It is a pleasure to meet you again, Elsa Grey."

Elsa blushed, remembering how she had practically run him over on their first encounter. "Yes, this is a much better way to meet."

Charles chuckled and agreed. He subtly sniffed the air. It seemed that whoever was approaching earlier had reversed. That probably meant that whoever it was meant Elsa no good. Why else would the person turn around as soon as he made his presence known? He glanced down at her, she was looking down at the water, as the ship propelled forward. He remembered his dream, of how he had felt her lips beneath his. He wondered if they were as soft and sweet as they had been in his dream. He inhaled sharply; he had to stay away from her. It was about time for her to go back to her cabin; he wanted to scour through the rest of the ship while most of the passengers slept. But, he didn't want to leave her alone. He hoped she would agree. "Maybe it's time you went back to your cabin," he suggested. "I think it's much safer for you there."

He let out a relieved sigh, when she agreed. "Yes, I think you're right. I've been out here long enough; I should be able to sleep now. Well, it was nice to meet you Charles, enjoy the rest of your night." Elsa turned to walk away.

Involuntarily, Charles reached out a hand to stop her. Startled she turned to look at his hand on her arm, her confused gaze then slid to his face. What the hell did I stop her for? "Uh, please let me escort you back to your cabin."

She smiled up at him, "Sure, I would like that." Elsa couldn't believe she had kept her cool and actually had a conversation with Charles like a normal person. Lisa was right; her people skills were definitely improving. She couldn't wait to e-mail her friend and share the good news. She stole a quick glance up at Charles. She couldn't get over how good looking he was! She couldn't believe her luck in getting such a chance encounter with him. They reached her cabin all too soon. She unlocked her door and turned to him, "Thank you for walking with me, you're very kind."

"No problem," he stood, not making a move; merely looking at her intently.

Elsa wondered why he was looking at her like that. She didn't have much experience with men. Ok I don't have any experience with men at all. Was he waiting for her to say something else? A slight feeling of panic began to arise; she had no idea what to do know.

He finally broke the silence, "Goodnight Elsa, I will see you around."

"Okay, bye," she rushed out and stepped into her room, closing the door softly. She let out a sigh and sagged against the door. Why did she have to be so damn awkward all the time? Okay, bye? She couldn't have come up with something better to say? Something sophisticated like "Would you like to meet for breakfast or dinner?" She hit herself in the forehead with her palm and walked over to her bed to throw herself down in frustration. With the amount of people on this ship, she didn't even know if she would see him anytime soon. I am such an idiot.

Charles stood on the other side of Elsa's door, in a haze of confusion. What was it about her that called to him? He'd had to use every ounce of his self-control not to pull her to him and kiss her. There was no denying it anymore, he wanted Elsa Grey. But he had to deny himself the pleasure of making her his. He couldn't pull her into his dangerous world. Besides, she would run screaming for the hills if she knew the dark secret he kept.

He fought the urge to knock on her door and ask her to meet him for lunch or dinner. Instead, he turned and walked away. It would be best for him to stay away from her. He had work to do before the ship became busy with activities once again. He walked just about every inch of the ship, trying to sniff out his adversary. He found nothing. Either the man had done a hell of a job of hiding his presence, or he wasn't on the ship at all. Frustrated, Charles went back to his suite. It was almost sunrise; he might as well get some sleep.

Shortly after falling into a fitful slumber, images of red hair and brown eyes swirled around in his mind. Erotic images of himself laying Elsa on his silk sheets and claiming her body as his took over his mind completely.

Elsa sat at the pools side, watching everyone around her enjoy themselves. She sighed; she wanted to enjoy herself too. It was the first and probably only vacation she would spend out of Georgia; and she hadn't done anything fun yet. It was only the second day of the cruise, but time was running out, she only had six more days to make this experience truly amazing. Maybe she should go to a party tonight. Yes, that is what she would do. She was going to get all dolled up and go to one of the many parties held on the ship. Perhaps she would make a friend or two. *Maybe I will run into Charles again.* She sighed, a girl could only hope. She had been disappointed when she hadn't spotted him anywhere in the morning. Her hope of seeing him was the only reason she was lounging beside the pool in her best swimsuit. Maybe he hadn't woken up as yet; he had been up very late after all.

"Hello there." Elsa looked up at the sound of a high pitched voice. A middle aged, portly woman in a large floral sun dress stood before her."

"Hello," Elsa replied with a smile.

"May I sit beside you, dear? My husband refused to accompany me this morning and I do so hate being alone."

Tell me about it, "Of course" she said pointing to the lounge chair beside her. She was relieved that someonewas talking to her. She had started to feel very awkward sitting by herself.

"Thank you; you're such a lovely girl. I'm Tabitha," the woman said reaching out her chubby hand for a handshake."

"Nice to meet you Tabitha," Elsa said taking her hand. "I'm Elsa."

Tabitha settled in, making herself comfortable. "How has your time on bard been so far, Elsa?"

"Uh, it's been okay."

"Just okay? A pretty young thing like you should be having more than just an okay time."

Elsa laughed, comfortable in the older woman's presence. "I came on this vacation alone, so I haven't really ventured out as yet. I guess if I had company, I would be having a better time."

"Oh but of course dear, going on a cruise alone is rarely any fun. The only plus is having the opportunity to find yourself a mate." Tabitha winked conspiratorially, causing Elsa to giggle.

The older woman was delightful. "I suppose you're right."

"Tell you what; why don't you have dinner with my Arnold and me tonight? We would be delighted to have you join us."

Elsa considered for a moment and agreed. She wasn't going to be picky when it came to friends; they was a rare commodity as far as she was concerned. "I would love to, thank you."

"Lovely, you can meet us in International Cuisine at seven. It seems you have an admirer, dear."

"Huh?" Elsa threw Tabitha a confused look.

"There is a man, staring at you from a cross the pool." Tabitha's nose wrinkled in distaste, "I must say, he isn't very handsome though."

Elsa followed Tabitha's gaze. She froze when she noticed who her 'admirer' was. Oh my God. It was the same thin, creepy man who had given her the chills yesterday. What were the chances of finding him staring at her again? Is he stalking me or something? Scared by the thought, Elsa decided that it was time to leave. "Uh, Tabitha I have to go now, but you will definitely see me at dinner. Thank you so much for the invite."

"Oh, okay dear," Tabitha said disappointed that her company was departing so soon. "I will see you later."

Elsa threw her a broad smile and scurried away. She looked over her shoulder to see if Mr. Creepy was still watching her, but he was gone. Who is he? She hoped he wasn't some pervert who preyed on young girls on vacation by themselves. She had seen something like that in a movie once. She shuddered at the thought. Just my luck to be stalked on my first vacation, she thought miserably. Maybe she should report the man to the authorities on board. But, he had only been looking at her, he hadn't really done anything. She would look foolish if she told anyone. She decided to hide in her room until dinner time.

If she was lucky, she would run into Charles Grimm again later. She grinned at the thought of seeing him again, and her stomach did somersaults. Oh, no I'm becoming obsessed with the man. Obsession was in no way attractive; she had to remember to keep her cool if she saw him again. She entered her room and headed straight to the balcony. She loved the view she had of the ocean. Staring into the blue depth, she wondered why she was getting so worked up about Charles. He probably wasn't even interested in her. He seemed like the kind of man who could have any woman he wanted. Her shoulders drooped in defeat, she wasn't one of those gorgeous, sophisticated women she suspected he would be attracted to.

She thought back on their previous encounters. The first day on the main deck when she had collided with him, it seemed like he couldn't get away from her fast enough. He had let go of her arm and hurriedly walked away as if he had heard that she carried some contagious disease.

Last night, he couldn't get rid of her fast enough. She sighed, who was she kidding? She didn't have a chance with a man like that.

At six forty-five, Elsa stood in front of the mirror, putting on the final touches of her makeup. She had curled and brushed her hair until it hung in waves around her face and shoulders, her makeup was subtle and natural except for her lips, which were painted wine red. She stood back and smoothed her olive green cocktail dress. It hugged her slight curves in all the right places and ended mid thigh to accentuate her slender legs. She completed her look with a pair of faltering, strappy heels. Perfect, she thought smiling at her reflection. She looked appropriate for dinner as well as a party later in the night. Provided her courage didn't fail her as the night went on. She grabbed a small black clutch and left her room.

Elsa entered the restaurant and glanced around the room, looking for Tabitha. It wasn't long before Tabitha spotted her at the door and jumped out of her seat to wave at Elsa excitedly. Elsa smiled and walked over to the table.

"My, my, Elsa you look absolutely stunning," she breathed. "You remind me of my younger days, when I could pull off a dress like that."

"Thank you Tabitha," Elsa giggled. "You are still a looker."

"Oh you flatter an old lady. Come, let me introduce you to my Arnie. Arnold, darling, this is the young woman I told you about, Elsa. Elsa this is my husband, Arnold."

Arnold stood up and reached for Elsa's hand. "It is a pleasure to finally meet you Elsa, my old lady here has been gushing about you all day." He planted a kiss on the back of her hand and took in her appearance from head to toe, "And I can see why."

Tabitha swatted Arnold's arm, "She's too young for you, and you're married!"

The couple laughed and Elsa couldn't help joining in at their easy humor. It must be nice to have someone to joke around with like that. Elsa gazed at them with longing; the older couple looked so happy together. Arnold politely assisted the women into their seats and took his own.

The threesome immediately erupted into animated conversation. Elsa was quite surprised at the ease with which she interacted with Elsa and Arnold. Her usual awkwardness and shyness had disappeared. Maybe I should stick to the older crowd, she thought. Or maybe she had underestimated her ability to connect with people.

Charles sat at the bar in International Cuisine. He had already downed a few drinks and was nursing another. He had thwarted a few women's attempts to engage him in conversation. Some had coyly tried to capture his attention while a few had blatantly flirted with him. He snorted at the memory of one woman who had wasted no time in asking him to take her back to his room. Apparently her husband was asleep in their cabin and wouldn't miss her for a few hours.

Charles shook his head; he should be used to female attention by now. The problem was, it was one woman's attention that he craved. Unfortunately, he felt like he had to avoid her for her own protection. He sighed heavily and took a sip of the strong liquor. He thought of Elsa, he liked being in her presence. Earlier when he had spoken to her on the main deck, he had felt a sense of ease and calmness. She was sweet and quiet; he smiled at the memory of her blushing several times. It was delightful to meet a woman who still blushed. The type of women he usually encountered were so money-hungry, they seemed to have lost their souls in pursuit of rich husbands.

He supposed he should be grateful for what he was. His need to protect his secret had forced him not to get too close to women. So, he was never at risk for being caught in their treacherous snares. His billions were appealing to many women; but the closest he ever got to any of them was to have a one night stand. Elsa was different; she was too innocent to hide the stars she had in her eyes when she gazed at him and she had no idea how much he was worth. Her genuine attraction to him was refreshing. His attraction to her was threatening to make him abandon all his good senses. He was tempted to go down to her cabin and make his feelings for her known.

As if he had magically conjured her up, the object of his constant thoughts walked into the room. The glass that he was bringing up to his lips paused in mid-air. Elsa looked absolutely beautiful, he watched as she stopped and glanced around the room. His heart dropped, was she here to meet a man? She had told him she was on the cruise alone, but a gorgeous girl like her could easily meet someone. If he had missed his chance, he was entirely to blame. He was the one who had been trying to stay away. Now it seem like some other lucky man had seized the opportunity.

She smiled brightly at someone across the room. He wished he was the one on the receiving end of that smile. Men turned to give her second looks as she passed. He gave a low growl, jealousy rearing its ugly head; he would like to break the necks of every man who lusted after her. The dangerous beast in him rippled beneath the surface; she is mine, it whispered, startling him. He took several calming breaths and took a long drink from his glass. His eyes never left her as she walked up to a middle aged couple. He let out a relieved breath and the beast in side of him instantly settled.

Charles jumped off of his stool, he needed some air. He walked outside quickly. Holy shit, he was just prepared to tear apart any man Elsa had been meeting with. What was the matter with him? He barely knew Elsa, he merely new that he was attracted to her. He had never felt the beast inside of him react out of jealousy before. He ran a hand through his hair. My God, it was almost like he was obsessed with Elsa Grey. He did not have the time to worry about such emotions now; he had other pressing matters to worry about.

Chapter Five

Elsa had enjoyed dinner with Tabitha and Arnold immensely. She found the older couple so endearing. They were like the parents she didn't have, she thought with a pang of sadness. She missed her parents so much; she had been such a happy child when they were alive. Tabitha and Arnold reminded her of what she was missing. They had shared amusing stories of their lives together. They had never had any children and Elsa thought they would have made great parents.

Throughout dinner, she couldn't stop her mind from wandering to thoughts of Charles. At one point, she thought she had spotted him with her peripheral vision. But when she looked around she had seen no sign of him. She decided that it was just wishful thinking. She had wanted to see him so badly that her mind had played a trick on her. She had battled with herself to put thoughts of Charles aside and focus on her dinner companions.

After dinner, she had said her goodbyes to Arnold and Tabitha and gone in search of more entertainment. She was determined to join the party scene tonight. She was going to shove aside her fears and let loose. If she partied tonight, at least she would have something exciting to tell Lisa. She will be so proud. Elsa followed the sound of pulsing music in the distance; she walked down the long corridor. The sound was coming from further away than she thought.

Elsa stopped to glance around as a cold feeling settled in the pit of her stomach. She thought she saw a movement in the shadows. She shook her head and laughed at herself. Why was she always letting her wild imagination get the best of her? Her recurring dreams came back to her. She was uncomfortable with the similarities between her dreams and this moment. She was always running down a passageway similar this one. It was highly unlikely that she would be attacked by an unknown entity with claws on a cruise ship full of people. As she approached the club, the sound of a blood curdling scream startled her, causing her to jump. It sounded like someone needed help.

Elsa walked toward the sound of the scream and found a group of people gathering around what appeared to be a person lying on the floor. There were muttered whispers and gasps, along with crying and swearing. What was going on? She pushed her way through the growing crowd, to find the cause of the commotion. As she got closer, her hand flew to her mouth; she inhaled sharply wanting to but not able to look away from the gruesome scene before her. A man's lifeless body sat slumped against the wall, his throat partially ripped out. Blood splattered the wall and the floor around the body.

"It looks like he has suffered some kind of animal attack," a male passenger observed.

"That is preposterous, there are no animals on this ship," a woman countered.

"Has anyone called the security personnel?" asked a newcomer.

Elsa backed away from the body, she felt as though she was going to be ill. She turned around and rushed down the corridor. She nearly collided with someone coming around the corner. "Elsa, what is it?" Charles asked. Unable to speak she pointed behind her and pushed passed him. He contemplated going after her to make sure she was alright, but he let her go. He had to deal with the situation at hand. She didn't have to tell him anything, he was well aware of what he would find up ahead. He could smell the blood from a mile away and hear the whispers of the crowd. Someone was dead, and there was talk of a wild animal.

Charles slowly walked toward the crowd of passengers. He assessed the ghastly scene before him. He inhaled sharply, he is here. His head whipped around to scan the crowd, looking for the man he suspected was the culprit of the murder. He wasn't among the crown. But, he had finally slipped up and Charles knew that he was definitely aboard this ship now. It seemed the murderer could no longer control the beast inside of him. Now everyone on board was in danger. Being in such close proximity to so many people was too tempting for their kind not to feed; which left Charles puzzled as to why the man was on a cruise ship in the first place. It made no sense. He extracted himself from the scene as crew members came rushing down the corridor.

Charles sniffed the air; he detected a faint scent of the animal and headed in that direction. The man he sought was known to him only as Victor. That was the name his father had whispered before he died. The memory of that night flooded Charles' memories. It was only two years ago, he had walked into his father's London home to find a man standing over his bloodied body. The man had looked up and Charles had gotten a good look at his face. The man had taken off, before Charles could react. He had chosen to remain at his father's side, rather than go after the intruder. His father was on the verge of dying; before he took his last breath he whispered "Victor wants the girl, he wanted me to tell him where she is."

Up to this day Charles had not figured out which girl his father had spoken of; but he had been tracking Victor ever since. The man was a as elusive as they came, it was difficult to get him cornered. This was the closest Charles had ever come to catching the man in two years. He stopped, could the woman that his father had spoken of be the reason for Victor's presence on this ship? Victor's faint remaining scent had lead Charles out to the main deck. He followed it to the rail and the smell ended abruptly. He looked over into the ocean, confused. The man couldn't have jumped overboard, could he? Once again, Charles had lost his Victor's trail. He growled in frustration, his eyes flashing a golden yellow. At least he knew he was on this ship.

Elsa had been violently ill after returning to her cabin. She had showered and replaced her dress with comfortable silk pajamas. The dreadful scene and the raw smell of blood still plagued her senses. Now she lay in bed curled up in a tiny ball, trying to rid her mind of what she had seen. How could something like that happen on a cruise ship?

Images from her recurring nightmare flashed through her mind. The shadowy figure with yellow eyes and claws swirled around in her head. Could her dream be real after all? She shuddered as she remembered the feeling she had gotten as she walked down the corridor in search of the party earlier. It was as though she had instinctively known something had been wrong, but she had shaken off the feeling and passed it off as her mind having been ridiculous. Could she have somehow saved that man's life? She thought she had detected movement in the corridor; it could have been the killer fleeing the scene.

She groaned; she didn't know what to think anymore. Now more than ever, she wished she didn't have to be alone. Elsa drew her pillow near and wrapped her arms around it in an effort to comfort herself. She glanced at the clock as her eyelids drooped. Five after one, I should get some sleep. Her eyes drifted closed. Soon she was caught up in a haze of her recurring dream mixed with images of herself in Charles' arms.

She woke up with a start to what sounded like scratching on her cabin door. She waited, listening to hear the sound again. It sounded as if an animal was scratching at her door, trying to get in. What the hell? She swung out of bed and padded across the carpeted floor. She pressed her ear to the door and waited, listening for the strange sound again. She didn't hear anything. She wondered if she was hearing things, it had been a traumatic night after all. She slowly pulled the door open and peered into the hall way. She knew very well that it wasn't the smartest thing to do, but her curiosity got the better of her. She detected a slight movement in her peripheral. Her head swung in the direction to see what it was, but there was no one there. "Hello? Who's there?" She called.

Elsa stepped out into the hall. *Apparently I've lost all good sense*, she thought. She knew the best thing for her to do was to go back to her cabin and lock her door. She had seen enough movies to know that she was being less than smart. Curiosity killed the cat, she reminded herself. But, she almost felt compelled to find out who was lurking around the corridor. She walked cautiously to the end of the hall. She didn't see anyone, so she turned to go back to her cabin. Something moved in the dark corner and she whipped around. "I- I know you're there. Why are you hiding? What do you want?" A thought occurred to her; it could be her creepy stalker hiding in the shadows; waiting for the right moment to grab her.

Her good senses seem to return immediately. Oh man, I should get back to my cabin. What had she been thinking, venturing out of her cabin? She was like a stupid girl in a horror movie; placing herself in danger, making it easy for the killer to get to her. Before she could turn and walk away, cold hands wrapped around her upper arm, pulling her away from the lit hallway and into a dark passage. She let out a scream and kicked hard, connecting with a body part. Her attacker hissed and loosed his grip, allowing her to make a run for it. She didn't get very far before her feet were kicked out from under her and a hand grabbed her calf and once again attempted to pull her into the shadows.

Oh my God, I'm going to be killed. She screamed, hoping that someone would hear and come to her aid. She thrashed and kicked violently, trying to break her attackers grip. Suddenly, the hand on her leg loosened and she quickly crawled into the lit passage way. There were thuds in the darkness, as if there was a struggle. Two bodies fell into the light and she instantly recognized one of them. Charles. He threw a punch, knocking the hooded man off of his feet; he regained his footing and set off in a run. "Elsa, are you all right?"

She remained on the floor, eyes wide in shock and terror, "I-I think so." He reached for her and helped her to her feet. "Thank you for saving me."

"What are you doing out of your cabin at this hour?"

She glanced guiltily at him, it was her fault she had been attacked. She should have stayed in her room. "Well, I heard a strange noise and I came out to investigate."

Charles gawked at her, unable to believe what he had just heard. "That was incredibly stupid of you Elsa, if you hear weird noises outside your door; it's none of your business. You're not a detective," he hissed.

Elsa frowned, she knew she had made a less than smart decision, but he didn't have to be so snippy. "I was curious and I thought maybe I could help somehow, to catch whoever killed that man." She hung her head, remembering the awful scene.

Charles sighed, "I'm sorry, I didn't mean to snap at you. Are you sure you're alright?" She nodded, "Come on, let's get you back to your cabin." He took her arm gently and led her down the hallway. Thank God I got here in time. Standing on the upper deck earlier, he had realized that Victor had probably jumped to a lower deck and not overboard as he had initially thought. He had searched every deck below, hoping to catch the bastard. Before he had reached this deck, Victor's scent had become stronger and he knew he was closing in on him. Then, he had heard a woman scream, and came running down the stairs at supernatural speed. As he neared, he had picked up Elsa's scent mingling with Victor's. Panic had almost seized him at the thought that she was the one being attacked Victor.

He couldn't let the fate that had reached that poor man earlier, reach Elsa. The beast in him had rippled, urging him to go faster. When he had seen Victor with his hands on Elsa he had almost lost his control, but reined his beast in; not wanting to expose his true nature to Elsa or anyone else who might be watching. They reached her door and he ushered her into the small space.

Elsa immediately walked to the couch and dropped down, her knees no longer able to support her weight. She couldn't stop her body from shaking. She had almost ended up being another murder victim. What the hell was happening on this ship? This paradise was quickly turning into hell on the blue seas. First she was stalked, next she saw a man ripped apart by God know what; and then, she was attacked. Elsa wanted her vacation to end right then, so that she could go back to Georgia and resume her boring life. She had a new appreciation for the dull life she had back home now. All of this was far too much excitement for her to handle. She wrapped her arms around herself and rocked back and forth, trying to stop the shudders that racked her body.

Charles moved to sit beside her on the couch. He tipped her chin up to study her face, "You're not alright; you're shaking like a leaf."

Elsa gave him a forced, weak smile "Almost getting killed will have that effect on you." His close proximity was starting to serve as a nice distraction from her trauma. "Do you think the same man that attacked me, killed that man?"

"I don't know," Charles lied.

"What happened after I left?"

"Some crew members along with the Captain came to investigate. The body was removed. When the ship docks in the Bahamas tomorrow; their authorities will most likely start an investigation."

She nodded; with all the excitement, she had forgotten that they were to stop on the island the next day. She was startled when Charles spontaneously wrapped his arms and around her and pulled her to his chest. She stiffened momentarily, but quickly relaxed. This was totally new to her; she had never been in a man's embrace before.

Charles rested his chin on her head, "You looked like you could use a little body heat, with all that shivering," he explained.

"Thanks," Elsa said softly.

Charles took a deep breath. She felt damn good in his arms, but he wanted to do more much more than that. He wanted to do the things to her that he had done every night in his dreams since the day he had met her. His gaze drifted to the bed and he pictured himself carrying her to it and laying her down. He inhaled sharply, trying to rid his mind of his carnal thoughts. He shifted beside her, suddenly unable to manage such close proximity to her.

She eased up to glance at him, "Are you okay?"

"Yes, I'm fine. It's just that I should get going."

"Oh, right. Okay," Elsa felt a pang of disappointment, as she sat forward to allow him to stand. He rose up and walked to the door; she followed behind him. Before reaching to open the door, he turned abruptly to her causing her to walk right into him. He quickly reached out to steady her. She took a step back and giggled, "We have got to stop meeting like this."

He smiled down at her, "I really don't mind at all." His gaze remained on her, making her feel a bit uncomfortable. She swallowed hard when his gaze lowered to rest on her lips. She squirmed, not sure what to do. She gasped softly when his head lowered and he captured her lips. Holy crap, she thought. She remained still, not sure how to react; in all of her twenty three years, she had never been kissed before. But, she had never admitted that to anyone. She was as innocent as the day she was born. The slight movement of his lips urged hers to move, and she parted them hesitantly. Elsa followed the motion of his lips, imitating his every move.

He bunched his fingers in her hair and she bought her hands up to rest on his chest. He deepened the kiss, tilting her head back for a better angle. She let out a soft sigh, which he captured in his mouth. She tasted like heaven. Her lips are as soft as I had dreamed, he thought. Her feminine scent infiltrated his senses; she was intoxicating. The beast moved inside him, ready to claim her. He couldn't let that happen, he was determined to keep her safe; even from himself. Charles reluctantly ended the kiss and put distance between them. Elsa stood gazing up at him, a little dazed.

Her fingers flew to her lips as if to keep the imprint of his lips there. Wow, if this was what kissing was like all the time, she had been missing out. She could have sworn she felt the earth move, which was ridiculous because they were on water.

"I-I'm sorry Elsa, I don't know what came over me."

She shook her head vigorously, "No, please don't apologize, that was nice."

His eyebrows shot up and his lips curled into a grin. She smiled back. "It was," he agreed softly. He had to get away from her before he ended up tearing her clothes off. He pulled open the door and stepped out into the hall way.

"Charles," Elsa called, causing him to pause and look back.

"Um, when we dock in the Bahamas later, would you like to hang out for a bit?" Elsa held her breath, waiting for his response.

He tilted his head and studied her, considering her invitation. He finally answered, "I would like that. Oh, and you looked ravishing at dinner with your friends, by the way. Lock your door; and don't come out until everyone else is up." He threw her a smile and walked away.

Elsa locked the door and leaned against it, clutching her chest. Her heart was doing back flips and she had to keep it from jumping out of her chest cavity. She smiled, so he had been in the restaurant. Her extra effort to put herself together had not been wasted after all, he had seen her; and he though she looked ravishing. Not only that, but they would be spending time together later. She clapped her hands in glee, squealing as she jumped on her bed. She was like a teenage girl, getting ready to go on her first date. Well, it was actually kind of her first date. A sliver of panic rippled through her. *Oh my God, is it a date? What is expected of me? What will I wear?* A million questions swirled around in her head, as she stared into space in abject horror. What if she ruined things with Charles, with her lack of people skills? Oh no, what had she been thinking inviting him out like that? In her moment of newfound boldness, she had not considered the consequences. She threw herself down dramatically, covering her face with her hands. *I can't cancel now.*

Charles stood in the shadows, watching Elsa's door. He was afraid Victor would return to finish the job. Why would Victor target her any way? It had to be a random attack. He decided that he wouldn't move until he knew it was safe for him to leave. He was going to spend the day with Elsa in a little while. He didn't know what had possessed him to accept her invitation; he was supposed to be avoiding her. But staring into her brown, hopeful eyes; he couldn't fight the compulsion to say yes.

His eyes flashed in the dark and his wolf surged with satisfaction. He groaned silently, how could he be with Elsa with the secret he held? He would have to hide what he was from her, which was the reason he hadn't wanted to get involved with her in the first place. Plus, being with him could potentially put her in danger. He did not want her hurt in any way. But, he could no longer fight the strong feelings he had for the woman. There was something special about her and he knew that if he let her go, he would never find another woman like her again. He sighed, his emotions in a swirl of conflict. Damn it. He was supposed to be focusing on getting rid of the threat to Elsa and everyone else on this ship. Instead he was standing in a dark corner watching the door of the object of his obsession.

Chapter Six

The ship finally docked on the beautiful island of the Bahamas. Elsa stood on the main deck with Tabitha and Arnold, watching as the ship crawled into the port. The older couple had taken Elsa under their wings. She had shared breakfast with them earlier and had remained on deck with them for the remainder of the morning. There was a round of applause and cheering as the ship came to a stop. Despite the tragedy that had taken place the night before, the passengers were excited to explore the attractions of the island.

To everyone's disappointment the Captain's voice resonated from the speakers, informing them that everyone had to stay on board until the Bahamian police ran an investigation of the mysterious death that had happened on board. There was loud roll of disappointed murmurs.

"Oh dear, I was looking forward to doing a little shopping on the island," Tabitha huffed.

"Maybe, after the police have done their jobs, we will get to leave the ship," Elsa suggested.

"I hope you're right, dear. We spent a lot of money on this cruise and I want everything that was offered out of it."

Elsa smiled sympathetically. She could understand how Tabitha felt, but she wanted the killer on board to be discovered. She could have very well been his second victim had it not been for Charles. Just the thought of his name caused her hear to flutter. She needed serious help. She had to e-mail Lisa to tell her about Charles, she thought excitedly. She had actually had her first kiss; of course, Lisa didn't need to know that it was her first. "Tabitha I need to run, there's something I have to do."

"Okay dear, just be careful. Weird things are happening on this ship."

"I will, I promise." Elsa took off and headed to the internet café. She exited signed in to her e-mail, her hands shaking in anticipation to share the events of the previous night with Lisa. First, she opened the response from Lisa and read:

Hey Elsa,

How are you girl? Don't worry; your vacation is bound to get more interesting. This guy you mentioned must be really hot. I have never heard you gush over any man. Don't think you've ruined things with him honey, you just met him. Just play it cool and be yourself. If this guy really likes you, he will show it. Miss you so much. Take care and I can't wait to hear from you again. Bye

Elsa smiled, Lisa was spot on; she had not scared Charles off after all. And her vacation had gotten more interesting, a little too interesting for her liking. She clicked reply and typed her message:

Dear Lisa,

You are absolutely right; my vacation is quickly becoming more exciting by the day. The guy I mentioned, his name is Charles Grim and he is wonderful. My attraction for him has grown to epic proportions. It looks like he is interested in me as well. He initiated a kiss last night; so that's a good sign right? We have just docked in the Bahamas; and Charles and I have plans to hang out today. I'm equally excited and nervous.

To add more excitement to the mix, there has been a murder on board. This vacation has taken a strange turn. I don't know any details about the tragedy yet, but I sure hope the police get to the bottom of it. Anyway, I will let you know about my day with Charles. Later.

Elsa sent the message with a huge smile on her face; she could imagine Lisa looking over her shoulder to make sure the boss wasn't coming so she could open her personal e-mail. She could see her friend bouncing in her seat with her usual excited energy as she read the message. She could wait to see Lisa's response. She had deliberately left out the part about her being attacked last and rescued by Charles. There was need to worry Lisa

As Elsa walked back to the main deck, she wondered if she and Charles' plan to hang out on the island would come to fruition. They were restricted from leaving the ship after all. Her heart sank in disappointment. She supposed she would just find Tabitha and Arnold and spend the rest of the morning with them.

A few hours later she sat at the pool side with Tabitha, sipping a cool drink and chatting about her years in college. "It seems you are full of admirers dear," Tabitha said, pointing her chin to the far end of the pool.

Oh no, not again. Her head whipped around expecting to find Mr. Creepy staring at her again. To relief and absolute delight, Charles stood sporting long shorts and a buttoned down shirt with a pair of sunglasses. His long hair was tousled by the wind, he looked amazing. He smiled broadly at her. She beamed, signaling for him to come over.

"This one is quite handsome dear," Tabitha whispered behind her hand and let out a girly giggle. "I had better keep my eyes to myself, my Arnie can be quite jealous you know."

Elsa smiled, fighting the urge to burst out laughing. Tabitha said the funniest things. "I agree, he is very handsome," Elsa whispered back just as Charles approached them.

"Good afternoon ladies," Charles greeted them.

Elsa could feel his gaze on her beneath his sunglasses. She blushed wildly, "Hi."

Tabitha sat up, "Good day, young man," she drawled, holding her plump hand out to Charles.

His lips kicked up at the sides in amusement, as he removed his sunglasses and took Tabitha's hand in his. He gave an elegant bow, "How do you do? I'm Charles Grimm the third," he planted a kiss on the back of Tabitha's hand.

Tabitha drew in an audible breath and clutched her chest with her free hand. She let out high pitched giggle "I'm Tabitha, it's a pleasure to meet you. I detect an accent. Where are you from?"

"England," Charles answered.

"Oh my, I do love a man with an accent."

Elsa watched the exchange in quiet amusement. Had Tabitha nearly swooned? She stifled a giggle. Her older companion was suddenly acting like a young school girl in the presence of a handsome, charming man. Elsa knew how Tabitha felt all too well as Charles had the same effect on her.

Charles continued, speaking to Tabitha "I am sorry to interrupt, but I would like to whisk Elsa away for lunch. Would you like to join us Tabitha?"

Tabitha looked from Charles to Elsa, something sparked in her eyes, "Oh no, you youths go on ahead, I want to stay here and soak up a little more sun in these old bones." She winked at Elsa.

Elsa took Charles's outstretched hand and stood up. "Enjoy the rest of your afternoon Tabitha. Are we still on for dinner later?"

Tabitha considered for a few seconds, "You know what dear; I think I want to stay in my cabin for dinner later and turn in early if we don't get the chance to leave the ship. I'm sorry to disappoint you dear; I'm not as energetic as you young people. Perhaps Charles can keep you company this evening." She looked up at Elsa innocently, who was still fighting not to giggle. Could Tabitha's attempt at matchmaking be any more obvious?

"Okay Tabitha, take care."

"See you tomorrow, dear!" she said as she waved them off.

Charles chuckled as they walked away, "I can see why you enjoy Tabitha's company; she is delightful."

"She sure is; her and her husband together are even more fun," Elsa said laughing. "I was a bit worried that our plans would be off for today, considering we can't leave the ship."

"We can still hang out on the ship; there are plenty of things to do on board. We can explore the island later, when things settle down."

Elsa smiled, "So where to now?"

"I'm starving, so let's find some food." Charles stole a glance at Elsa; what he really craved was her. She looked delectable in a pair of white shorts that left gave a nice view of her shapely thighs and a pink tight tank top that hugged the slight curve of her breasts. He realized that she wore no bra underneath and swallowed hard. She was going to drive him mad.

The entered the first restaurant they spotted and seated themselves. A waiter came over and quickly took their orders. As they sat waiting for their meal, Elsa took a deep breath and struck up a conversation, "So, are you enjoying the cruise so far?"

He considered for a minute, "I am now."

She smiled shyly, her lashes lowering in an attempt to hide her pleasure. "So am I." She glanced up at him, "What bought you all the way from England?"

An unidentified expression crossed his face, but it quickly disappeared and he gave a slight smile. "I was in the states on business and I happened across the brochure for this cruise. I figured I needed a vacation; and here I am." He felt bad for blatantly lying to Elsa, but there was no way he could tell her the real reason he was on the ship. He imagined telling her that he was hunting a wolf shifter, one like himself. She would most likely get up and run away, screaming that he was insane. He needed to shift the focus from himself and on to her. "Tell me a little bit about yourself Elsa."

"Well, there is nothing very interesting to tell."

"Start with where you grew up," he suggested.

"Well, I grew up in Pennsylvania. I went to college in Georgia and I decided to stay there after I graduated."

"Why did you end up going to college so far from home?"

Sadness flashed in her eyes, "I wanted to get away from the place where I had so many bad memories." Elsa was surprised that she had volunteered that piece of information. It seemed she was quite comfortable talking to Charles.

Charles wished he could take away her sadness, he knew what it was like to run away from bad memories. "What happened, if you don't mind me asking?"

"I lost both parents when I was nine and then I moved in with my uncle. Let's just say he wasn't very good with children. I was pretty much isolated as a child."

"I'm sorry; every child deserves a happy home."

She sighed, "I think so too."

"Where is your uncle now?"

"He died a few weeks ago. I have no family left. I feel so alone sometimes."

They had much in common; he was the only surviving member of his family too. Victor had taken the only person he had left two years ago. He felt alone in the world as well. "I lost my family too."

She smiled sadly at him and nodded in understanding. They enjoyed the rest of their lunch in a comfortable silence; both admiring the ocean view from their window seat. At the end of lunch, Charles made a surprising invitation. "Would you like to come back to my cabin?"

Elsa gaped at him for a moment, and then quickly snapped her open mouth shut. "Uh, sure."

He smiled and rose from the table; he held his hands out to her, "Great, let's go."

She placed her hand in his and willingly followed. At this point, she felt like she would follow him anywhere in the world. She was a bundle of nerves by the time they reached Charles' cabin door. She had no idea what she was doing; or what she should do when she went inside. He opened the door and allowed her in. Wow. His cabin was fancy. It looked like it cost a lot of money. "Make yourself comfortable," he said pointing to a large couch across from a king sized bed."Would you like something to drink?"

"Water please." That's what she needed to soothe her suddenly parched throat. She wished she had more experience with men. She wanted to be poised and nonchalant like the sophisticated ladies she saw on television. When Charles walked away to retrieve the drinks, she quickly smoothed her hair and checked her teeth using the shiny surface of the glass coffee table in front of her.

Charles came back with a glass of water and handed it to her. "Thank you," she said, turning the glass to her head for a long drink.

Charles gave a slight smirk, he could detect her nervousness and he found it endearing. Attempting to put her at ease he moved away from her to switch on the television. "I figured we could hang out in here, for the rest of the afternoon. I don't like crowds very much."

Elsa relaxed visibly, "Neither do I, I'm not very good with people."

"You seem to be doing just fine to me."

She beamed at him, "Thanks, you're very sweet."

His eyebrows rose in amusement, he let out a low chuckle, "I have never been described as sweet before."

Elsa blushed, "Well, I think you are," she said softly. "I like that about you, Charles. I like everything about you." Her pulse rate picked up speed as she made her admission. She swallowed hard and glanced at him beneath her lashes. She boldly decided to cease the moment and let him know how she felt.

Charles inhaled sharply, he considered lying to her. He really should tell her that he didn't feel the same way she did; get rid of her for her own good. But, the lie couldn't come out. "I like you too Elsa. I have been fantasizing about you since you bumped into me on the first day."

She stared at him, happy and amazed by the words coming from his mouth. Thank God he felt the same way. She didn't know if her self-esteem could handle rejection after the first time expressing her feelings to a man. "You have no idea how relieved I am to hear that."

"Come here, Elsa," he commanded.

The steely undertone in his voice sent shivers down her spine. She put her glass down and got up, slowly obeying his command. She slowly sauntered to where he sat on the edge of the bed. Elsa stopped in front of him, wondering what she should do next. He simply looked at her with an intensity that ignited something deep within her. Her knees quivered and her breathing quickened; he hadn't even touched her and she was melting at his feet. The effect he had on her was something she couldn't fathom. Charles snaked his hands around her slender waist and gently pulled her to stand between his legs. He looked up at her with a mixture of amazement and confusion. "I don't know what it is about you Elsa, but I just can't seem to stay away; no matter how hard I try."

She tilted her head and frowned, before she could ask him why he tried to stay away from her; he covered her lips with his own and all other thoughts were wiped from her mind. He tilted his head back, providing her with better access to his mouth. Her hands rested on his broad shoulders and she stepped even closer to him between his thighs. His large hands slipped beneath her top, making contact with her skin. An electric shock ran through her entire body at the skin to skin contact. She could tell by his sharp intake of breath that he felt it too.

Without breaking the kiss he made a swift movement; she was surprised to find herself lying on the bed with him stretched out beside her. He released her lip to stare in to her brown eyes, she wasn't sure what he was searching for; but it seemed that he found it because he bent to continue his sensuous assault on her body. He feathered kisses on her neck, moving down to her breasts. Charles gave a slight tug at her top and her breasts sprang free. He covered one nipple with his mouth. Elsa gasped and arched her back, nearly jumping out of her own skin. Motivated by her reaction; his hand inched its way down to the waistband of her shorts. He undid the buttons, sliding his hand inside.

Elsa's thighs clamped closed. Startled, his gaze swung to her face, "I'm sorry. Am I moving too fast?"

She shook her head vigorously, "N-no, it's not that at all. It's just... I want to, but I've never..." Her cheeks flamed, and her lashes lowered to hide her embarrassment. She couldn't seem to get the words, that she was a virgin.

Charles stared at her in confusion as he tried to make sense of her jumbled words. Then understanding suddenly dawned on him; his eyes widened. Oh. "Elsa, are you trying to tell that you have never had sex before?"

She groaned throwing her hands up to cover her flushed face. "Yes Charles that is exactly what I was trying to tell you. I'm twenty- three years old and I' still a virgin. It's okay if you laugh." She opened her fingers to peek at him. He gazed down at her with a slight smile. He doesn't seem freaked out, she thought.

She was younger than he thought, seven years his junior. Pure male satisfaction coursed through Charles, at the discovery that he would be the first to claim her. And the only one, his wolf whispered. "There is nothing wrong with that Elsa; as a matter of fact I am pleased that I will get to give you your first lesson." He seized her lips, cutting off her response. Now that her secret was out and Charles was okay with it, Elsa felt a surge of courage. She wrapped her arms around his neck, crushing her body against his. The feel of his rock hard chest against her soft breasts drove her wild.

Charles resumed his earlier task; shifting to lay beside her, he slid his hand inside her shorts once again. He wanted to get her ready before he took her completely. His fingers brushed over her sensitive bud and she gasped and stiffened. She had never felt anything like that before. "Relax for me Elsa," he whispered. She relaxed against him, trusting him completely. He slowly eased one finger into her tight passage. She moaned, "Charles." He continued his assault. He pushed into her again, adding another finger; all the while massaging her sensitive nub. Pressure started to build in her core, a sensation that she wasn't familiar with washed over her. Soon the tightness building up inside of her released and pleasure rocked her entire body. "Oh my God, Charles!" Her body lifted off the bed; if he was not holding her, she suspected her body would have lifted to the ceiling. She lay breathing hard, unable to believe that something could feel so good.

Charles gazed down at her. Elsa coming undone with pleasure in his arms was the most beautiful thing he had ever seen. He craved that reaction from her again. He began to undress her; he could wait no longer, he wanted to feel what it was like to be inside of her. A loud knock sounded at the door. Elsa jumped, her hands flying up to cover herself. Damn it, he thought. This had better be important. He walked to the door and hauled it open in frustration, "What?" He growled. A male employee stood cowering at the door.

"S-sorry to bother you sir, but you are now free to leave the ship. There isn't much time though, the ship will be leaving port at eight-thirty tonight. I'm sorry again sir." He quickly scurried away, to knock on another door. Charles closed the door and released a sigh. The man couldn't have come thirty minutes later? He muttered a curse.

"Well it looks like we are free to go," he said to Elsa who was standing beside the bed adjusting her clothes. The mood was now gone. Maybe it's for the best, he thought. Maybe he shouldn't get any closer to her.

"That's great," she said, avoiding his gaze "We can go and see a little bit of the island."

"Sure," he responded. "Let's go."

Chapter Seven

Charles assessed the crowd gathered on the main deck of the ship. It was almost time for the ship to set sail once again. He had spent the past three hours exploring and shopping with Elsa and her elderly friends. He glanced down at Elsa, she was chatting animatedly to Tabitha about the beauty of the island they were about to depart from. He wondered if Victor was hiding in the crowd. He sniffed the air but couldn't pick up the man's scent. An array of perfumes and other scents from the crowd assailed his nostrils instead.

Elsa stole a quick peek at Charles; he had been quiet since they had left the ship. He still had not said much. Her fingers fiddled with the necklace around her neck. It was a gold chain that held a single green, oval gem. It had captured her attention; he had caught her admiring it. "Why don't you pick it up?"

She had shown him the price tag, "I can only admire it from afar."

"I'll pay for it."

"Oh no, I can't let you do that Charles. It's pretty, but it isn't something that I need. Come on let's find Tabitha and Arnold, it's almost time to board the ship."

He had hesitated for a moment, "You go ahead; I will join you in a little bit." Charles had waited until she was out of sight before picking up the necklace. He had paid for it; and she'd had no idea until he had presented it to her at the dinner table. Elsa had refused to accept it, but he insisted. Tabitha had chimed in, "Take it, dear, it's gorgeous. You've got yourself a thoughtful and romantic man; just like my Arnie." Arnold had beamed. Elsa had given in and accepted Charles' gift. She was in love with the necklace. It was extra special because of who she had got it from.

Now, Elsa frowned; she was concerned. Why had Charles been so quiet? He seemed distracted as well. He had not been behaving like that earlier when they were in his cabin. She blushed as she remembered their time together earlier. Desire rushed through her. She was well aware that they would have ended up having sex, if they had not been interrupted. Was that the problem? Was he upset because they had not gotten to finish what they started? But, he had bought her a lovely, expensive gift; so he couldn't be mad at her, right? She cursed her inexperience when it came to men. "Charles, are you okay?" she asked, finally.

He glanced down at her, "Of course, why?"

"You seem a little distracted."

Before he could answer, there was an eruption of noise. Passengers celebrated as the ship move away from the port. "Here's to four more days of paradise!" A man shouted, holding up a glass. There was a loud chorus of agreement from the crowd. Elsa clapped along with everyone else, all the while eying Charles with unease.

Hours later Charles sat on his bed, brooding in silence. Elsa sat with her head rested against the headboard of the bed, studying him. He had invited her back to his room; and she had been thrilled. It meant that he wasn't upset with her and probably wanted to continue where they had left off earlier. But he hadn't made a single move toward her. His behavior was way too confusing. What should she do? Was she no good at relationships? Is this even a relationship? She wondered. They had only known each other for three days; and it wasn't like they had actually slept together. She sighed loudly, capturing his attention. He turned to her, "Are you okay?"

"No, I'm not."

He frowned in confusion, "What is wrong?"

She scoffed, "You are what is wrong, Charles."

"What the hell are you talking about?"

"You've been acting strange all evening; all quiet and distant. Have I done something wrong?"

"No, of course not; I just have a lot on my mind." She remained silent waiting for him to continue. How could he tell her that he was worried that the other wolf shifter on board would take another life? He had insisted she come back to his cabin, in order to keep her safe. He wasn't going to let her out of his sight for the remainder of the cruise.

"Well, aren't you going to tell me what's on your mind?"

He sighed, "Forget it, it's nothing important."

"Obviously it is, if it has consumed your mind all evening."

"Let it go, Elsa!" He growled.

Taken aback by his menacing tone, she scooted off the bed and headed to the door. "Maybe it's best if I go back to my cabin. It seems you need some time alone."

"Elsa, get back here," he growled again.

Her eye brows shot up, "Not with that tone, I won't," she snapped and pulled the door open. Before he could respond, she slammed the door and stomped off. How dare he speak to her like that? Her lips trembled and her eyes shimmered with tears. She didn't know much about the dynamics between men and women; but she was well aware that he had no right to speak to her like that. She hadn't done anything to deserve such a tone.

Charles threw his head back in frustration, damn it. He had not meant to take his frustration out on Elsa. He gave himself a hard mental kick in the ass. He jumped up off the bed; he had to get her back in here for her own safety. He opened the door and went after her. He spotted her getting in to the elevator. "Elsa, wait!" He called, running to catch the door before it closed.

Elsa saw him coming; but she didn't want to talk to talk to him. She pushed the button, to speed up the closing of the elevator door. The door slid closed before he could get close enough to hold it. He muttered several curses and headed for the stairs. Charles was leaning against the wall waiting for the elevator to arrive on the lower deck. "How did you get down here so fast?" She asked.

"Don't worry about it."

She glared at him and walked past him, lifting her chin in disdain. "You are mighty rude this evening," she muttered.

He sighed heavily and reached out to take hold of her arm, "I know, and I'm sorry. I didn't mean to raise my voice at you."

She wheeled around to face him, "Just tell me what's wrong, Charles" she implored.

"I'm just worried."

"What are you worried about?"

He searched for a way to explain, but not give too much away. "I've just had a bad feeling all evening, that something bad is going to happen."

"Well, that's awfully vague. Care to be a little more specific?"

Before he could answer, he caught a whiff of something in the air. His lips curled into a sneer. Victor. He nearly bared sharp teeth, but remembered that Elsa was present. He released a low growl.

"Charles, what is it?" Elsa asked, suddenly afraid of the feral gleam she saw in his eyes. Did he just growl? He wasn't looking at her; instead he was searching the corridor for God only knew what. She followed his gaze in confusion. What was he looking? "For God's sake Charles, what is the matter?"

"Elsa, I have to get you out of here," he took her hand and dragged her back up the stairs. They entered another empty corridor and move toward the back of the ship.

Elsa struggled to keep up with him. "Charles, stop. Who are we running from?" He stopped abruptly, turning around. He shoved her behind him, "Elsa run," the deadly tone of his voice stopped her from questioning him. She gulped and slowly backed away. A man appeared out of the shadows. Elsa recognized him as the man who had been stalking her, Mr. Creepy. His eyes flashed yellow. Elsa gasped loudly; it was just like in her dream. How was that humanly possible?

"Elsa, I said run," Charles hissed. The man rushed toward Charles. Elsa turned around and did as she was told. She didn't stop running until she reached the back opening of the ship. She had to get help, that man looked like he meant to do Charles harm. She looked around. There was no one. What if Charles was hurt? She had to go back and help him. Just as she turned to go back inside, a figure jumped in front of her. The man reached for her, grabbing her by the neck. She kicked him in the shin with every ounce of strength she possessed; he released her in surprise. She crumpled to the floor as Charles came running out. Mr. Creepy was nowhere to be seen. She was relieved that Charles was not hurt.

He spotted her on the floor and rushed to her. His detected a new scent, causing him to swing around. "What the hell- his words were cut off as the unknown man attacked him, hitting him in the chest with clawed hands. He hit the floor with a loud thud, the air knocked out of him. Using his super strength he shoved the man, sending him flying backward. Charles tried to get a look at the new adversary's face but he wore a black mask over his face. There is another shifter on the ship? Why hadn't he detected this one before now? The man hissed and rushed forward again, this time going for Elsa who was now on her feet. She saw him rushing toward her and quickly backed away. Realizing that she had no further to go, she stopped; eyes wide in terror. The last thing she saw before her attacker shoved her overboard, was Charles running toward her; terror evident in his eyes. She let out a scream as she tumbled over the rail.

"No! Elsa!" Charles watched in sheer horror as she fell overboard. The masked shifter turned and sprinted towards him, knocking him off his feet. The only thing on his mind as he hit the floor was Elsa. Had he lost her forever?

Deadly Secrets
Part 2: Secrets Revealed

Chapter One

Charles landed on his back, hitting the ground with a loud thud. The air was instantly knocked out of him. He lay still for a moment, not able to breathe. *Elsa.* He had lost her. Pain ripped through him. He thought of letting his adversary take his life. What was the point in fighting? The one person that he had found a true connection with was gone. Elsa had bought color to his grey world. He was all alone, once again; first his father and now Elsa. The thought of returning to a lonely existence was not appealing to him. He watched as the masked figure ran toward him. He still wondered who was beneath the mask. It was evidently another shifter, but why wasn't his presence known before tonight? The ship had left port three days ago and this mystery shifter was never once detected. He was good at hiding his presence. Charles wondered if he was in league with his nemesis, Victor.

His mind stopped racing, stopped trying to find answers. None of it mattered now; he shut his eyes tightly. This was it, he decided to let go. Just before the man pounced on him, Charles heard a soft cry. *Could it be?* It came again.

"Charles!" Elsa cried, her small voice carried by the wind as the large cruise ship sliced through the dark water. Charles's eyes sprang open, *Elsa.* It could be his imagination, because he wanted so badly for her to be alive. It didn't matter in that moment. The sound of her sweet voice, even imagined, gave him renewed motivation and sprung him into action. He rolled to his left dodging the masked figure as he jumped aiming extended, sharp claws at his chest. The man grunted in frustration when he realized he missed his target and spun around, preparing himself to attach again. Charles jumped agilely to his feet and crouched, ready for the next attack.

"Charles, help! I'm slipping!" Elsa's voice sounded again. *It really is her.* Relief flooded through Charles' entire being. He had to get rid of his adversary and get to her. The urgent need to get to Elsa bought the beast inside of him to the surface. His hazel eyes flashed a golden yellow and his fingers transformed into lethal claws, ready to shred his enemy to pieces. He gave a low menacing growl as he set his eyes upon the masked man with deadly purpose. This was the man who had attempted to take Elsa away from him. With that thought he lost all control and the wolf within him took over, momentarily making him more animal than man. His attacker raced toward him and he took off to meet him half way.

Both men pounced, meeting in the air, claws clashing. Charles's talons struck flesh, digging into the man's chest, creating a long gash. The masked man hissed in anger and pain. He looked down at the gaping wound on his chest, and hesitated; pondering if he should strike at Charles again. A growl rumbled in Charles's throat, daring his enemy to make another move. The unknown man's eyes flashed in the darkness, his fist bunched. He could not meet Charles's challenge. He decided against retaliation and turned, fleeing in to the darkness of the ship, leaving a trail of blood as he ran.

Elsa hung on for dear life. She had been pushed overboard by someone wearing a black mask. The scene had played out just like the nightmares she had been having for the past few weeks. She was chased to the end of the ship in the most recent version of her nightmare. Only in her dream she woke up just as the shadowy figure rushed toward her. Her worst dream had just become reality. She held on tightly to the edge of the ship's floor. She slowly peeped down, whimpering in fear at the sight of the imposing sea below her dangling feet. The blue pristine water had been made black by the darkness of the night. Her fingers slipped slightly and panic rose up in her chest. Oh no, she didn't know how much longer she could hold on; and worse she didn't know how to swim. If she lost her grip, she would surely drown. *Why didn't I learn how to swim?* She made a mental note to sign up for swimming lessons, if she survived. Although, her chance of survival was looking pretty slim at the moment.

Her fingers slipped again, "Charles help!" She wondered if he could hear her. What if he was hurt or worse? She prayed he was alright. Her arms began to burn and tremble from holding her body up for so long; her fingers were starting to feel numb. She cursed herself for having never subscribed to a gym. If she was in better shape, she would be able to hold on much longer. *Oh God, I'm going to die.* Her life flashed before her eyes. She was never going to see Lisa again, her only friend; just when their relationship had really started. She was never going to see Charles again; never get to explore her feeling for him. She thought of how close they had come to making love. Now she wished they had, it would have been her first experience. She was never going to get that experience. *It's just my luck to die a virgin,* she thought.

She couldn't hold on any longer. She closed her eyes and prepared herself to hit the cold, black abyss. She took a deep breath, ready to meet her end. A warm hand clamped around her wrist, her eyes flew open and she looked up to see Charles. Her hear soared, he had come to her rescue once again. She was glad to see that he was unhurt. "Charles," she whispered his name as if it was talisman.

"I'm here." He anchored himself with his free hand and slowly pulled her weight upward, until she was standing beside him. He assisted her over the rail then climbed over himself. Elsa collapsed on the floor, her breathing laboured as she thought of how close she had come to dying. Charles instantly pulled her up and into his arms. She wrapped her hands around him tightly, still shivering from her brush with death. "My God, Elsa I thought I lost you." He broke their embrace to hold her at arm's length. His gaze swept over her from head to toe. "Are you alright?"

Elsa struggled to get her word out. "I-I think so. I almost died. I thought I was going to fall to my death for sure." Shudders rocked her entire body and the tears she had been holding back began to flow. Loud sobs came from deep down. She cried because she had been so afraid; and because she was relieved that she was still alive. Charles pulled her back into his arms, resting his chin on the top of her head. He drew in a deep breath, taking in her essence. He wanted to keep her in his arms forever, never let her go. The shivers ripping through her body, forced him to let her go. He had to get her inside, away from the cool night breeze.

"Let's get you inside," he whispered. He kept one arm around her waist to support her. It seemed as if her knees could not hold her body upward, they shook uncontrollably. Elsa walked beside him. Her arms wrapped around her middle, trying to stop herself from shaking. Her knees finally gave way. Without breaking his stride, Charles swept her into his arms. She wrapped her aching arms around his shoulders and buried her face in the crook of his neck.

"Who was that man, Charles? The one that attacked us?" She asked in a small voice.

"He ran off."

Her head lifted slightly so she that she could gaze at him, "Just like that?"

"Uh we fought for a bit."

She stopped to look at him, "Oh my God are you hurt?"

"I'm fine. Goodness you're shaking like a leaf." He carried her through the empty passage way. "I'm taking you back to my cabin and that is where you will still until this ship docks. I'm not letting you out of my sight Elsa. There is no telling if our mystery man knows your cabin."

Elsa nodded; she could not agree more. There was no way she was going to stay by herself. She was relieved when they finally reached Charles's cabin. As soon as they entered the room, Charles placed her on her feet and began to undress her. "W-what are you doing?"

"You need to take a warm bath," he said, concentrating on his task.

Elsa blushed; it was new to her to have a man undress her for a bath. "Oh ok," she said threw chattering teeth. Charles stripped her down to her underwear and she blushed even harder. "Sit," he indicated her to the bed. She ambled over on shaky legs and plopped down. He disappeared into the bathroom to fill the bath tub with warm water. A few minutes later he returned and reached for her hand. "Let's go."

She took his hand and followed him, on wooden legs to the luxurious bathroom. "Your bathroom looks way better than mine." Elsa stood in the middle of the room, admiring the fancy set up. "I'm coming up here to use your bathroom from now on," she teased.

He grinned, glad that she was able to joke about something. "You are more than welcome." Charles reached for Elsa, startling her. He unhooked her bra and slid it off her shoulders. Her sheer panty came next. She swallowed hard, embarrassed that he was seeing her naked. Her hand flew self-consciously to cover herself. He reached for her hands and pulled them away. "You don't have to hide from me Elsa," he said softly. "I have already seen you naked. Get in the tub." She slowly stepped over and sat in the warm water. She breathed a sigh as the warm water engulfed her body and she stopped shivering.

She glanced up at him, "You were right, I needed this."

He gave a slight smile, "I'll wait for you in the bedroom." He reluctantly turned to walk away. He wanted to keep her in his sight at all times. It had destroyed him when he thought he wouldn't see her again.

A soft, shy voice stopped him, "Charles, wait." He turned to look at her. "Don't leave. Join me." Elsa surprised herself. Perhaps it was her near death experience that had bought on her new found boldness. The Elsa she knew would never have invited a man into the tub with her.

The corners of his lips kicked up slightly, "I'm glad you asked. I would love to." She watched in fascination as he removed his clothes.

Elsa gasped when she saw a long red mark across his left shoulder. Blood had dried up around the gash. "You're hurt."

He glanced down at the wound and shrugged, "It's just a scratch." It had been way deeper when Victor had struck him in the hallway. But his kind had the gift of accelerated healing. The scar would disappear in no time, leaving no trace that he was ever injured. He stepped in tub and Elsa sat forward to accommodate him. He stretched out his legs around her and pulled her back to him. She relaxed against him, closing her eyes.

"Did I thank you for saving my life? That makes two times in three days, you deserve a medal; and I need to just stay in locked room for the rest of the cruise."

He chuckled, "You don't have to thank me for saving your life." He shuddered at the memory of her flipping over the ship's rail. The terror that he had felt in that moment was unlike any had ever felt before; and he had faced some terrifying enemies in his time.

"What happened to the man in the hallway, Mr. Creepy?" Elsa remembered the way his piercing blue eyes always bore into her. She had caught him staring at her strangely on several occasions. She was convinced he was stalking her, hence his nickname.

Charles didn't want her to know too much. He had delivered Victor a deadly blow to the neck. The man had clutched his neck and staggered away from him. The only thing that had saved Victor was his need to find Elsa; so he had left the man alive. When they had walked back to his cabin, there had not been any sign of Victor. So, that meant he was still alive. It was a pity he did not bleed to death, that would take one problem off of Charles's hands. "He uh... he ran off as well. I injured him." He quickly changed the subject, "What kind of name is Mr. Creepy? I doubt that is his right name."

Elsa laughed. "It's a nickname silly. Don't you England folks know anything about nicknames? I call him that because I swear the man has been stalking me since I boarded this ship."

Charles stiffened, "What do you mean he's been stalking you?"

"Well, it could be my imagination or just random coincidence but a couple times I have caught him staring at me. Just standing there, not even blinking. It creeps me out, hence the name Mr. Creepy. The way his eyes dig in to me is very disconcerting." Elsa shuddered remembering how the man's blue eyes seemed as if they could see into her very soul.

Alarmed, Charles gripped her shoulders and turned her slightly to him. "Why the hell didn't you tell me Elsa?"

She whipped around in the tub, her eyes flying to his; startled at his sudden aggression, "It just never came up." She winced as his fingers dug into her shoulders, "Ouch, you're hurting me."

He instantly lightened his grip, "I'm sorry." He gently rubbed the prints of his fingers marring her pale skin.

"What's with you anyway?" Elsa asked confused. It's not like he could have done anything about it. "I don't have any proof that the man has been stalking me, just a few weird encounters."

"I guess I'm just feeling overprotective after everything that transpired tonight, that's all," he muttered. Elsa turned back around and relaxed against him once more.

Elsa relaxed, "Thanks, I like the idea of having a protector. You're my knight in shining armour."

Charles's brows furrowed. Why would Victor have any interest in Elsa? She was a girl from Georgia. What possible connection could she have to Victor or any of his kind? The mysterious masked shifter had also gone after her. It had to be some random coincidence. He just could not put together any connection between Elsa and the other shifters. He stiffened again after a moment. There was a connection. *Me.* He knew he should have stayed away from her. He had bought her into his world. Now she was in danger by just being with him. He cursed himself mentally. If only he had been strong enough to walk away from her, she wouldn't have been put in danger tonight. He sighed. *Damn it.*

"Are you ok?" Elsa could feel the tension in Charles's body all of a sudden. She craned her neck to look at him. He seemed troubled.

"I'm fine. I'm just upset that your life was endangered tonight."

"It's not like it's your fault, Charles."

"It just might be," he muttered.

"What do you mean?"

"Uh, I have made some enemies in my time." Elsa frowned, confusion written on her face. She waited for him to explain. "I um... I may have rubbed a few business competitors the wrong way, to make the amount of money that I do. You just never know what some of those shrewd business men are capable of doing." Charles felt terrible for lying through his teeth, the story he had just concocted was a load of crap. But, he had no choice. He could not tell Elsa the truth about what Victor and the unknown masked man was. He could tell her what *he* was.

Elsa took his hand in hers, "It's highly unlikely that any of your business competitors would go through the trouble of following you on a Caribbean cruise just to get back at you. I have merely been in the wrong places at the wrong time and I randomly got attacked twice. Besides, it's not like I was a target, if you will recall, somebody else was murdered. There is just a criminal on this ship targeting innocent people."

Charles wrapped his arms around her and rested his chin in the crook of her neck, "Maybe you're right." But he knew better.

Chapter Two

Elsa lay on Charles's bed watching him as he poured wine in to a glass. She followed his every movement; admiring how the muscles of his arms bunched. The wine glass looked small in his large hand. He presented her with the half full glass. "Here this will help you to relax."

She took the glass gratefully, "Thank you." She needed something to settle her nerves, after the night she'd had. She took large gulps until the glass was empty. She might just need the entire bottle of wine. She held the glass out for more. Charles obliged by pouring more into the glass. He watched in amazement as she rapidly emptied the glass once again.

Charles pried the glass out of her fingers, "Ok, I think that is quite enough for now, young lady." He rested the glass down and climbed into the bed beside her. He wanted to go out and search every corner of the ship for Victor and the unknown shifter before the ship came alive with activity, but he was reluctant to leave Elsa alone. He pulled her into his arms and fixed the sheets over her. She rested her head against his chest.

Charles was amazed at how much he had come to care for the red haired woman in his arms. He recalled the first day of the cruise, when she had collided into him on the main deck. He had instantly felt the current between then on physical contact. His feelings for her since then had bordered on obsession. His attraction for her was felt down to his very core, even the animal in him was enamoured with her. His father had once told him, when he was younger, that every wolf had his true life mate. The bond between true life mates could be felt; and became more powerful with intimate joining. Could Elsa be his true mate? But he was also told that a male shifter's life mate was found among his same kind. Elsa was not a wolf shifter. Were there exceptions? He had no idea. All he knew was that he wanted to make

Elsa his, and he would kill whoever tried to take her from him. His wolf rippled inside of him in agreement.

Elsa's eyelids drooped and she stifled a yawn. Exhaustion swept over her. "I'm glad I met you Charles. Meeting you is by far the best thing that has happened to me on this vacation,' she said sleepily.

He smiled, "I'm glad I met you too." He tipped her chin up with his finger tips and lowered his head to cover her lips with his own. Her lips parted and he deepened the kiss." He reluctantly pulled away, inhaling deeply. "You need to get some sleep, you look exhausted."

"Of course I do, I haven't slept properly in weeks."

"Why is that?"

"I've been plagued with nightmares." Elsa's head popped up "As a matter of fact, everything that happened tonight played out almost like my dream. In my last nightmare, something stalked me from the shadows and I ran to the back of the ship. This shadowy figure with yellow eyes and claw came after me, but I woke up before it got hold of me." Elsa stopped as memories of the night flashed through her mind. She shook her head, "No, it's not possible."

"What are you talking about?" Charles glanced down at her.

"I don't want to sound crazy."

"I won't think you're crazy, tell me."

She hesitated, "Well, I could have sworn that the man we encountered in the hall had yellow eyes." She shook her head and giggled. "But that's ridiculous, right?"

Charles stiffened, "Right, it is possible that it was just the reflection of the light." Elsa opened her mouth to comment, but he placed a finger on her lips. "No more talking, you need to sleep."

She sighed, "Ok, you're right." Elsa nestled against him and relaxed. Her eyes fluttered closed.

Charles lay still, with Elsa in his arms. Her breathing soon slowed and became heavy. She had fallen asleep. He stared up at the ceiling. He had lied to her once again. He sighed; she really had seen Victor's eyed flash yellow. He gave a low groan; how many more times would he have to lie to her? He stifled a yawn. His exhaustion had finally presented itself. He closed his eyes and drifted off to sleep.

Elsa stood at the end of the ship's deck. She watched in terror as the masked man rushed to her, hand outstretched. He gave one push and she stumbled over board. She grabbed on to a ledge just in time, stopping her from falling into the sea. *Not again*, she thought. Her fingers slipped from the ledge. She couldn't hold on any longer. She looked up to see Charles reaching down to her. She reached one hand up to grab his hand but her own hand slipped off the ledge. She let out a terrified scream as she fell into the deep sea. Her body hit the water and engulfed her.

Charles shook Elsa's shoulders as she screamed and thrashed about. She was caught in the throes of another nightmare. "Elsa, wake up you're dreaming." Her eyes flew open; her breaths came out in labored gasps. Charles gently wiped at the fine sheen of sweat on her forehead. He pulled her quivering body closer to him.

"Oh God, I really need swimming lessons," she blurted out.

"What?"

"Huh? Oh I-I it was just another dream." Charles held her as the shudders rippling through her subsided and her breathing slowed.

"Are you ok? You were screaming."

"Oh, I'm sorry I woke you."

"No need to apologize. What were you dreaming about?"

Elsa sighed and rubbed a hand over her face. When were the nightmares going to stop? They were starting to get really old. "I was reliving the incident from earlier. The only thing is, I actually fell into the water in my dream. And of course I can't swim." She gave a nervous giggle. "I probably should have learned how to swim before coming on a cruise right?"

He grinned down at her. He stroked her hair softly, "Lot of people can't swim. Maybe I can teach you."

"That would be nice."

"Tell you what, how about I give you a few lessons before this cruise ends. We've got three more days."

"We have a deal, Mr. Grim." Elsa's heart dropped, her time with Charles was quickly winding down. The ship would make another stop on the Berry Islands the next day. Then it would return to Miami. She probably wouldn't see him again.

"Why the sad face?"

"It's nothing; I just need to get some much needed sleep."

Elsa slowly came awake. She stretched feeling much better. She had not had another nightmare since falling back asleep and she felt more rested. *Sleeping in Charles's arms does wonders.* If only being wrapped in his embrace could last forever. But, she knew it couldn't. At the end of the cruise, they would part ways. They were after all from two different worlds. She turned her head to find Charles staring down at her intently. *Oh no, I must look terrible.* She fought the urge to reach her hand up and smooth her down her hair. But, she couldn't make it look too obvious. "Morning," she said softly.

He gave her a smile, "Good morning, beautiful. How did you sleep?"

"Pretty great; can we just move your bed down to my cabin and you take mine?"

He chuckled, "I have a simpler solution. You can just stay in here with me for the remainder of the trip."

Elsa's eyes widened, "Oh, are you sure you wouldn't get tired of me?"

"Never, I think it's a brilliant idea. Say yes." He grinned broadly, waiting for her to respond."

"Uh, ok." Wow she would practically be moving in him for the remainder of her vacation. "Lisa would be so excited if she knew about this," she muttered under her breath.

"Who is Lisa?" He asked.

She hadn't expected him to hear her. "She's my friend and co-worker." She glanced at him and continued to speak. "She is just about the only friend I have back in Georgia." She didn't want to talk about her life. She glanced at the clock. "Wow I can't believe I slept so late, it's almost eleven." She scooted off the bed. "Breakfast time, my body demands sustenance."

He smiled, "My stomach agrees."

By the time they made their way up to the main deck, it was after twelve. Elsa held on to Charles's hand, following him to one of the few restaurants on board. She stole a glance at him. She was amazed at how handsome he was. She counted herself so lucky to have met such a man on her first vacation. She glanced at their entwined hands. *So this is what it's like to be in a relationship*, the thought. She had no previous experience. They reached a table and Charles let go of her hand to pull a chair out for her. She smiled. "Thank you." *What a gentleman.*

Charles took his own seat. His gaze swept over the occupants of the restaurant. Now that he had the scent of the third shifter, he had discovered was on board, it would be easy to pick him out of a crowd. He was still puzzled. Where had he come from? How had he remained hidden for three days? The cruise ship was small and only held about two thousand five hundred people. He must have been deliberately hiding his presence; that was the only explanation. So, he must have known that he was not the only wolf shifter on boar. He nearly sighed out loud. Now he had two adversaries to deal with. He would have no conflict with the third shifter, but he had attempted to kill Elsa, that was enough to mark the man for death.

"Who are you looking for?" Elsa's question bought him out of his deep thoughts.

"I'm looking for any sign of our friends from last night."

Elsa glanced around. She leaned forward and whispered. "Don't you think we should report what happened last night? Those men could very well target someone else."

Horrified, Charles shook his head vigorously, "No there is no need for that yet."

"But, Charles they tried to kill us and one of them could be the culprit for the murder that took place on board the night before. Hell, they both could have teamed up to commit the murder. The authorities had no evidence to place the crime on anyone, so the murderer or murderers are running around free as birds. We could put an end to it."

"We don't have any solid evidence that either of the men from last night committed the murder, Elsa. We can't just go around accusing people of such a crime."

Elsa sighed and sat back, she was still convinced that they should report last night's incident. "Ok, fine."

Charles was relieved that she let it go. But, he had a feeling he would hear about it again. "Let's just enjoy breakfast."

Elsa threw him a suspicious glance. Why wouldn't he want to report the incident? It was clearly the most logical thing to do, so at least some investigation could take place. He had almost seemed nervous when she had mentioned reporting it. She looked back at last night. It was like he had known someone was coming after them, but she had not seen anyone in sight. He said both men had run off when he fought back. Was he part time wealthy business man and part time ninja or something? She shook her head and focused on her plate. She was just over thinking things.

Charles stole glances at Elsa. He wondered what she was thinking about. She had gone silent and was pushing around the food on her plate instead of eating it. He stifled a groan, she was a smart girl, and she would start to see cracks in his stories pretty soon. How much longer could he hide the truth from her? The thought of her running away from him if she found out the truth was enough to make him lose his appetite. He pushed his plate away; his wolf moved inside him, it hadn't gotten anything substantial to eat since the ship had left Miami. But Charles had great self control; he didn't feed off of or kill humans. He resigned himself to watching Elsa who had finally began to eat her food.

"Are you ready to return to my cabin?" He asked after she had finished.

Elsa wrinkled her nose, "Already? It's only one o'clock."

Of course she wouldn't want to be holed up in his cabin for the remainder of the cruise. What was he thinking? She was on vacation, she would be looking to have fun. He just wanted her safe and out of sight; but, he couldn't tell her that. "Ok, what would you like to do?"

"How about the swimming lessons you promised?"

He smiled slightly, "Sure. Why not?" What he would really love to do is take her back to his cabin and give her an entirely different lesson; one that involved his king sized bed and any other surface that could be used. He forced his mind away from his carnal thoughts. He would be sure to embarrass himself with an obvious erection when he stood up.

She beamed, "Great, but first I need to stop at the internet cafe. I have to e-mail Lisa."

"You can call her if you like. Use my cell."

"No way, that is way too expensive."

He chuckled, "It's nice of you to be concerned, but I can afford it."

Elsa's eyebrows rose; right he was a billionaire of course he didn't have to worry about the expense of making phone calls from a cruise ship."Ok, I would love to actually get talk to Lisa."

"In that case, follow me ma'am." She took his hand and followed him to his cabin.

"Lisa, Hi. Its Elsa." A loud shriek sounded over the phone. She had to hold it away from her ear to avoid permanent damage to her hearing.

"No way! I can't believe you're actually calling. How are you?"

"I'm fine. I'm glad to hear your voice."

"How are you calling? Isn't it way expensive to make calls from a ship?"

"Yes, but Charles offered me a call, he said it was ok."

Lisa gasped, "Oh it sounds like you and Charles are pretty tight."

Elsa looked around to see if Charles was in hearing distance. He was outside on the balcony looking out. "I spent the night in his cabin."

Another excited shriek sounded, "Oh my God, did you two have the sex?"

"Well no, not yet. We did come pretty close though. We would have if we hadn't been interrupted. I think it might happen soon though...I hope so." Elsa wanted to ask Lisa for a few pointers, because she was way in over her head. But, she refrained from letting Lisa know that she was completely inexperienced. It was just way too humiliating to admit. Although, Charles knew that she was a virgin and he didn't think anything was wrong with that. As a matter of fact, he had been pleased.

"When is going to happen? You need to speed things along, time is winding down."

"Ugh I know, don't remind me." She hated thinking about her limited time with Charles.

"Anyway, guess who had been asking me about you?"

"Uh, I have no idea." The only person she talked was Lisa.

"Jonathan! Yup he is still hot for you girl. I was tempted to tell him you are otherwise occupied with much bigger fish." Lisa giggled at her own humor.

Elsa dropped her head in her hand. "*Lisa*," she moaned.

"Relax I didn't say anything, I swear."

"Why doesn't Jonathan just leave me alone for Christ's sake. I thought he would get tired of my lack of response to him by now, and move on to someone else?"

"You obviously have what he wants honey," Lisa replied, chuckling.

Elsa rolled her eyes, "Well I don't want to stay on the phone too long. Charles said not to worry about it, but I still don't want to take advantage. It was really nice talking to you. I can't wait to get back so we can hang out and chat."

"Me too, Elsa. I miss you; just a few more days to go though. You stay safe and take care."

"You too, Lisa. Bye."

Elsa hung up the phone, smiling from ear to ear. She loved talking to Lisa. Just then Charles came back inside the cabin. Observing her face splitting grin he said, "You look happy."

"Oh, I'm always happy when I talk to Lisa. I think mentioned to you before that she is my only friend back in Georgia. She took the time to crack the shell I was encased in. I was terrible at interacting with people; I barely spoke two sentences to anyone. Until Lisa came along and showed me that maybe I had a sociable streak. She's great; I wish you could meet her."

Charles shot her a grin and moved to pour himself a glass of vodka. He downed the drink in one gulp; the liquid burned its way down his throat. He really needed to contain his anger or rather his jealously. He had not intended to eavesdrop on Elsa's conversation but his acute hearing could not help but pick up a few details. *Ok one particular detail.* He had tried to tune out Elsa's and Lisa's voices and words out of respect; until the mention of a name. *Jonathan.* Who was this Jonathan and what was his involvement with Elsa? "Who is Jonathan?" He blurted out.

"Excuse me?" How did he know about Jonathan? She gasped and threw him an accusatory glare. "Were you eavesdropping?"

He shook his head in denial, "No, I... I just heard the name that's all. I've never heard you mention anyone in your life but Lisa so I'm just curious as to who Jonathan is. Is he another good friend of yours?"

Elsa folded her arms. "He's my supervisor. Apparently he's interested in me but, I never realized until Lisa pointed it out. I never really paid him any mind." She wondered what else he had overheard. She hoped he didn't catch on to the fact that she had been taking about having sex with him. Elsa closed her eyes, humiliated at the thought.

"I see." Charles poured another drink and downed it one swallow. He felt a little better knowing Elsa only had a working relationship with Jonathan. That means he didn't have to make a stop in Georgia, find Jonathan; and rip his bloody head off. His wolf moved inside of him; loving the violent thoughts and the image of spilled blood.

"Are you ok Charles?" Elsa asked, concerned by his silence.

"Yes, ready to hit the pool?"

She smiled, "I am."

"Great, let's go."

Chapter Three

Elsa kicked around the pool, holding on for dear life to a flotation device. She groaned; she knew she must look absolutely ridiculous. She looked over at Charles and gave a weak smile. He stood close by smiling at the adorable picture she made. He couldn't remember the last time he had done something like this; playing around in a pool. His lived a serious, sometimes dangerous life. Elsa bought joy and laughter to his world. He nodded his encouragement and she continued at her task, her auburn hair glistened in the sun. "You're doing just fine," he called out.

"I'm feeling a bit tired, can I stop now?"

"Sure."

She threw him an uncomfortable look, "Uh, a little help." She was afraid if she stopped kicking, she would sink into the water.

Charles chuckled, "You can just stand up, you're feet will touch the bottom."

"Huh? Oh ok." She stopped kicking her feet and cautiously felt for the bottom of the pool with her feet. Relief washed through her when she felt the solid bottom beneath her feet.

Charles hopped out of the pool and stood up at the edge, waiting for Elsa to join him. He watched her make her way to him slowly; she threw him a smile. His breath hitched in his throat at the sexy sight she made. Her dark green bikini clung to her body, revealing tempting areas of skin. Her wet hair clung to her head and she reached up to sweep the wet mass to the side of her head. The slight motion lifted her breasts provocatively. She reached the steps of the pool and walked up, her hips swaying sensuously. He swallowed hard, and inhaled deeply. He wanted to take her back to his cabin immediately.

He reached his hand down to her and she took it, stepping up out of the pool. She giggled, "I am entirely hopeless. I don't think I will ever learn how to swim."

He threw a large towel over her shoulders. "It was only your first lesson. We can try again, "he encouraged.

Elsa moaned loudly, looking crestfallen at the idea. "Um, we will see." The side of his lips kicked up at her obvious reluctance. "I felt so foolish, kicking around like a child having to use a floatation device." She wished she'd had someone to teach her how to swim when she was younger. Painful memories of her childhood pushed into her mind. She had lost her parents as a child and had no one but her cold uncle; who had pretty much ignored her very existence. She had grown up alone and without love. Elsa's lashes lowered in an attempt to hide her pain.

Charles tipped her chin up with his fingers, "What's the matter?"

She raised her eyes to look at him, giving a sad smile. "It's nothing," she lied.

His eyebrows kicked up, "It doesn't look like nothing."

"Um, just childhood memories, that's all."

He detected her reluctance to discuss things any further and changed the subject. "Ok so what next?"

"I'm not really in the mood to do anything else, but relax a bit back in the cabin. We can come back up for dinner in a few hours."

"You got it, let's go." He took her hand, relieved that she wanted to go back to the cabin. He hated the idea of mingling among the crowd, especially with Victor and the mysterious shifter lurking around. They made their way across the main deck. Charles shot threatening glances at a few men who felt the need to give Elsa lingering and appreciative looks. He peeked at her; she stared ahead, complete oblivious to the attention she was receiving. His feelings of jealousy and possessiveness receded as they reached the empty corridor.

Elsa walked along side Charles. She glanced at him out of the corner of her eye. She wondered if he would finally make love to her once they were alone. She had found herself fantasizing about it several times. After the preview she had gotten the other day, she wanted to experience everything. She anticipated it. But he had not made another move toward her since then. She suddenly became alarmed; what if his mind had changed and he no longer wanted her? Her heart crumpled at the thought. She still very much wanted him. Lisa's words echoed in her head; she had to make it happen soon, her time with him was quickly winding down. "We will be stopping at the Berry Islands this evening, and then we're off to Miami. Our vacation is quickly approaching its end."

He glanced at her, "Yes, perhaps it for the best; with all the murders taking place."

"Perhaps." Her shoulders sagged; she didn't want it to end because that meant the end of her time with him. They approach his cabin. Elsa took a deep breath, trying to build up her courage. "Charles?"

"Hmmm?"

It was now or never, "Have you had any thought of uh... me lately?"

He frowned in confusion," What do you mean?" He refrained from telling her that she was constantly on her mind. But, he did not want to make his obsession of her known.

"Well not me, I really should say us." This was more difficult than she thought. She knew absolutely nothing about making the first move. She cursed her lack of experience. "What I'm trying to say is, we didn't get to finish what we started before we docked at the Bahamas the other day." As she finished her statement, Elsa's cheek flamed. She knew her entire face and body must match the shade of her hair. She averted her gaze, afraid to see his reaction. What if he laughed at her? In that moment, she wished the ground would open up and swallow her. At least she would be put out of her misery.

Understanding dawned on Charles. Near his cabin but he stopped walking, forcing her to stop as well. He pinned her with his gaze. "I'm painfully aware that we didn't, "he said softly; remembering that they were interrupted just when he was about to make her his. "To answer your question, I think about *us* very often."

"Oh," she gazed up at him, unable to say anything else.

"Are you saying you're ready to finish what we started, Elsa?" Before he finished the question he had her backed against the wall, his gaze penetrating her; waiting for her response.

Elsa's breath hitched. Her tongue darted out to moist her dry lips. His eyes followed every movement of her tongue. She swallowed hard, flustered at the hungry gaze her pinned her with. Her lashes lowered as she built up her courage; then her gaze slowly lifted to his. "Yes," she whispered.

He stared at her intently for a few seconds. Elsa nearly melted into a puddle at his feet. His stare alone, caused heat to rise in her. She watched in anticipation as his head lowered toward her. He was going to kiss her right there in the corridor. Her eyes darted around to make sure they were alone. His lips captured hers and she instantly forgot about anyone else. Her eyes fluttered closed as his lips move slowly over hers. He maneuvered them into a corner out of sight; but, they could still be seen by anyone who walked close enough. The chance of being discovered, served to excite Elsa even more. Charles pinned both of her wrists above her head with one hand and flicked the towel off her shoulders. It fell to the ground with a soft thud. His free hand cupped one of her breast and massaged gently, sending desire coursing through her. She moaned softly against his lips.

He pulled away to stared down at her. She met his gazed and held it as his hand roamed down her abdomen. Her breathing quickened when his hand brushed the inside of her thigh, then upward to run over her mound. He found the string at the side of her bathing suit bottom and began to slowly pull it loose. Her eyes widened; *oh my God, we're going to do it here.* Elsa felt a mixture of fear and excitement. Someone could pass at any minute and discover them.

His lips kicked up into a wicked grin at the shocked expression on Elsa's face. He wanted to take her right then and there, but his hand stopped before he could loosen her bathing suit. He inhaled sharply, what had gotten into him? This would be her first time; he couldn't take her against a wall, for goodness sake. He closed his eyes and shook his head, bringing back his rational thoughts. The woman drove him to madness. "What's wrong?" Elsa asked softly.

"This is your first time, Elsa. I want to make it special."

She visibly relaxed. For a moment she thought he had changed his mind. She smiled shyly at him, "It will be special as long as it's with you Charles."

Before he could respond, a scream echoed in the distance. Footsteps could be heard approaching. Charles reached down to retrieve the towel and covered her with it. The watch as another passenger ran past. "Someone help!" Elsa looked up at Charles wide eyed. He took her hand and pulled her from the corner. He led her to his cabin and opened the door with his key card. Gently pushing her inside he said, "Stay here, I'll be right back."

Elsa gasped, "No way, I'm coming with you."

"We don't know what danger is down there Elsa."

"Oh, so it's ok for you to walk into danger?" She glared at him.

He cocked an eyebrow, "Will you quit being stubborn and just do as I say? Please."

She rolled her eyes, "Ugh, fine," she hissed. He pulled the door closed. Elsa stood staring at the door, seething. Why was it ok for him to walk into potential danger? She appreciated his desire to protect her, but at the same time she wanted to protect him. He had come to mean so much to her in the short span of time they have been together. She could hear multiple footsteps running pass the door. She reached to open the door but dropped her hand. If she went outside, Charles would be angry. But her curiosity soon got the best of her and she pulled the door open. She followed the passing passengers and crew members down the corridor, wrapping the towel more tightly around her shoulders. A few moments later a small crowd came into view. Elsa tried to peer around bodies to see what was happening. Was that blood she saw on the floor? She ducked, pushing her way through the crowd.

She gasped, covering her mouth at the grisly sight. A woman laid face down, her hair spread out around her like a curtain, matted with blood. Her clothes had long shreds in them as if she was attacked by something with claws. Elsa's dream flashed through her mind, she was always chased by something with claws. She remembered the gash she had seen on Charles's shoulder. He must have gotten it in his fight with... *Mr. Creepy*. He had to be the culprit. Her eyes darted around, to see if the man was among the growing crowd. Her heart began to race as she remembered how he had come after her and Charles in the corridor the night before. The man was a vicious murder and he was running around free on the ship.

Oh my God, I could be next. Elsa knew he had her in his sight; he had come after her already; but she had escaped his clutches, thanks to Charles. Maybe he would try again. She felt ill at the thought that she could be the one lying on the floor lifeless in a pool of blood. She backed out of the middle of the crowd, her breathing labored. What if he was watching her now; waiting for the right moment to strike? She paled and stumbled backward. She backed right in to a hard chest; startled she whipped around. She let out a relieved breath when she saw that it was Charles. He was glaring daggers at her. She gave a slight shrug. "I wanted to see what was going on, "she said weakly. She was on the verge of fainting. A girl could only take so much blood and death.

Charles's anger turned to concern at the sight of her pallor. She swayed slightly. Was she going to faint? He took arm. "Elsa, take deep breaths."She looked at him feebly and took several deep breaths. "And this is why I told you to stay in the cabin. Come on; let's get you away from here." She followed him silently, but her mind was racing. If they had reported last night's incident, maybe this senseless murder could have been avoided. Things were escalating out of control. Who would be next?

Elsa's mind suddenly drifted to her friends, Tabitha and Arnold. She had not seen the couple all morning. After what she had just witnessed, she felt a pressing need to see them. She looked at Charles, "I need to check on Tabitha and Arnold."

"What? Right now? Elsa, I want to get you back to the safety of the cabin." He glanced around anxiously. He had caught Victor's and the mystery shifter's scents mingling with the other passengers. They were nowhere in sight, and not being able to see them was made him nervous.

She tore her arm from his grip, "Yes, right now. I'm going with or without you." She rushed passed him.

He grabbed her arm again before she got any further. "No, you can check on them later."

"Let go," she hissed. "You're not the boss of me." She yanked her arm free again.

"Elsa, if you don't listen to me, I will throw you over my shoulder."

She whirled around to face him, anger radiating from her. She balled her fist, ready to give him a piece of her mind. But, all of a sudden the energy seeped out of her. Her shoulders sagged and she looked at him defeated. "Will you just back off and let me go, Charles? After-after all that has happened, I just want to make sure they are ok."

The tears glistening in her eyes were his undoing. His resolve instantly weakened. He nodded, "I'll go with you." Elsa didn't reply, she turned and walked off. He followed behind her silently, his senses on full alert for any sign of a threat.

Elsa knocked on Tabitha and Arnold's door. It wasn't long before Tabitha crack the door open to peep out. She beamed at the sight of Elsa, flinging the door open. "Elsa dear how nice to see you." Elsa rushed into the older woman's arms. Tabitha's chubby arms instantly wrapped around her; her eyes flying questioningly to Charles. He remained silent. When Elsa finally let go of Tabitha she invited them inside. "What is the matter dear? You look upset."

Elsa wiped at her eyes, "I'm sorry for just showing up like this Tabitha. I just wanted to make sure you and Arnold are alright. I didn't see either for you down stairs as usual."

"Don't apologize Elsa, you're always welcome. Arnie has been feeling a bit under the weather since last night, so we stayed in today." She peeped around the corner, "He's asleep now."

"Oh no, I hope he feel better soon," Elsa said softly.

Tabitha studied Elsa for a few seconds, "No tell me what else has you upset."

Elsa ran a hand through her damp hair, "Another body was just found, a woman." Elsa stared into space, "She was just lying there in a pool of blood."

Tabitha clutched her chest, "Another one? My goodness that is just terrible. What in the world is going on?"

Elsa shrugged, "I heard murmurs of a wild animal. Both bodies showed signs of some kind of animal attack."

"But where would such a dangerous animal come from on a cruise ship, for goodness sake? It makes no sense."

"I know. But maybe you and Arnold should stay put in here until we reach the Berry Island. This ship isn't safe anymore."

"That is good advice dear. You two should do the same." She glanced at Charles, "You be sure to care of our girl now, Mr. Grim."

Charles nodded, "I will."

Elsa gave Tabitha another hug, "I'll see you later Tabitha. Please tell Arnold hello for me, when he wakes up."

"I will my dear. You take care now."

Charles let out a relived breath when he closed his cabin door. Some of the tension seeped from his body. He had been on high alert, ready to pounce at any inkling of danger. The knowledge that Elsa was in danger because of him was driving him mad. He needed a strong drink. No, he needed several strong drinks. He blew out another breath and wiped a hand over his face. Elsa glanced at him, "Are you angry with me?"

He sighed and shook his head. He busied himself pouring out the much needed liquor into a glass. He downed the liquid and poured more into the glass.

"If you're not angry, why are you not talking to me? Look, I'm sorry for losing my cool earlier. I just really needed to check on Tabitha Arnold." She paused, "I've just really come to care so much for them. They took me under their wings; and I suppose I see them as the parents that I lost."

"I understand Elsa, I'm not upset. Honestly." He turned to look at her. "Seeing that lifeless woman, just made me want to hide you from any danger that's all."

She gazed at him, I know, thank you. I've never had anyone care for me like that. I'm so use to being on my own and taking care of myself." She stood up and walked to him, taking the glass out of his hands. "I'm extremely grateful. Now tell me, what has you so on edge? I know it's more than a need to protect me."

Charles glanced at her. *Crap.* Elsa was finally seeing those cracks. She was starting to realize something else was going on. There was no way he could tell her what was really going on. "I just... I need some rest, my nerves are shot." Her hurt expression ripped him apart, but he still couldn't reveal anything more.

"Don't you trust me enough to tell me what else is bothering you?"

"Of course I trust you, but there really isn't anything else going on."

Elsa sighed, she wasn't born yesterday; she knew he was lying to her. "If you say so, Charles." She turned and walked away.

"You're angry with me."

Well aren't you observant, she thought sarcastically. "I'm fine. You don't have to tell me anything you don't want to. I'm going to get out if this damp bathing suit." She disappeared into the bathroom. A few minutes later he heard the shower running. He picked up the glass and took another shot of alcohol. *Damn it.*

Chapter Four

The cruise ship finally docked at the Berry Islands that evening. All passengers were gathered on the main deck and informed that they would remain on the Island until an investigation into the latest murder done. Everyone would be accommodated elsewhere on the island until further notice. Loud murmurs rippled through the crowd. Questions filled the air. "Where on this small Island can accommodate two thousand people? How long will we be stuck here? Will we get our money back for this ruined vacation?" Elsa stood silently, as the questions went on and on. She was leaned over the rail of the ship, staring into the distance.

Charles glanced her way. He groaned inwardly, she had not said a word to him after she had come out of the shower. She wouldn't even look at him. She seemed lost in thought. He would give his billions to know what she was thinking about. He was tempted to ask her, but abstained from doing so. He knew he was not her favourite person right now. He understood how frustrating it was to have someone constantly lying to him. His father had done so for years; hesitant at every opportunity to tell Charles what he really was. Growing up, he always knew something was off about him. When he confided in his father, he had always fed him nonsense about going through different phases. He had always known the old man was lying mercilessly. So, he understood if Elsa hated him at the moment.

Tabitha interrupted Elsa's thoughts, "Well, we had better pack everything we can; it seems we won't be able to come back on the ship once the investigation is underway."

Elsa nodded her agreement. "Let's get to it. I'm brining everything, just in case." They parted ways and agreed to meet up on the main deck. Tabitha expressed that she wanted to keep Elsa close. Elsa made her way to her cabin, with Charles close at her heels. "There is no need for you to accompany me. Don't you need to go and pack your things?"

"I told you I wasn't going to let you out of my sight. When you are done packing, you can wait for me in my cabin while I get a few things."

Elsa glowered, "Yes sir, you are the boss," she shot sarcastically. Charles said nothing, but cocked an eyebrow at her. She pushed her cabin door open with more force than necessary and stomped inside. She didn't know why she was so irritated with him. She knew he wasn't obligated to tell share his personal business with her. She supposed she was behaving like a sulky child. But, she noticed how stressed he was; and she cared so deeply for him. She just wanted to help him through whatever he seemed to be going through. Yes, weird and dangerous have been things have been happening; and that would add stress to anyone's life. But she knew there was more to his story than he was saying; it was extremely frustrating. She finished gathering her things in record time. She actually wanted to get off the ship as soon as possible, it now represented death and darkness in her eyes.

She followed Charles to his cabin and waited patiently as he packed a bag. "Ready?" He asked. She nodded. He threw id bag over his shoulder and bent to pick up hers.

"It's ok, I can carry it. It's a bit heavy."

"Its fine, I've got it. Let's go." When they reached the main deck, passengers were already exiting the ship.

Elsa stopped, "Let's wait a bit. Tabitha and Arnold haven't come down yet." Charles made no complaint; now knowledgeable of how attached Elsa had become to the older couple. They didn't have to wait much longer. Five minutes later Tabitha appeared, struggling with a huge bag; and Arnold followed closely behind, hauling a huge suitcase. As they came closer, Arnold could be heard muttering something about women and their habit of over packing. Elsa hid a smile and reached for Tabitha's bag.

"Oh thank you darling. Don't strain yourself now."

"It's not too heavy," Elsa lied. She wondered if Tabitha had somehow been able to pick up their entire cabin and stuff it into the bag. They fell into line with the rest of the passenger who were filing off of the ship. Elsa took a last look back before steeping off of the ramp. She could only hope there was enough evidence could be found to lock Mr. Creepy away for the rest of his life.

The large group was led to large empty hotel. The native islander that led them to their accommodations explained that the hotel was recently built and had not had the chance to open for business yet. It was sure to house everyone since many couples would and families would be sharing rooms. No had any idea f how long they would have to stay.

The crowd gathered in the lobby of the hotel, some spilling out on the front steps and of the building. The persons who required single rooms were asked to step forward. Elsa took a step forward. Charles quickly pulled her back to his side. "No you don't, we will share a room."

Elsa shot him startled glance, "Uh, we will?" He nodded grimly. Tabitha cleared her throat gave her a knowing look; while Arnold coughed behind his hands. Elsa flushed a bright pink. She stifled a groan; she wanted to die from embarrassment. Even though Charles had offered to let her stay in his cabin on the ship, she was not expecting him to want to share a room here. She remained silent until they were directed to their room.

Elsa looked around the sparsely furnished room. They were not yet open for business so she understood the lack of furniture. There was only a huge bed and dresser in the big pace. "This island beautiful, don't you think?" Elsa asked excitedly.

Charles was startled by the sound of her voice; he had not expected her to start talking to him again so soon. "It is," he agreed. "I believe The Berry Islands is composed of a string of thirty Cays, it is a part of the Bahamas. We are now on Great Harbor Cay."

"Wow, thirty? I had no idea."

"Most of them are inhabited." Charles's mood lightened somewhat. Even though they were just making small talk about geography, he was happy Elsa was talking to him.

Elsa walked to the window, "I wish we had gotten here earlier, so I could do some sightseeing. But, it's too dark now."

"We can go tomorrow." He didn't really want her to go out, for her own safety. But, he would have agreed to anything to make her happy at the moment. "I'm glad you're talking to me again," he confessed.

She turned from the window, "I realized that it was foolish of me to be upset with you. You're business is just that; your own. I have no right to demand anything from you." She lowered her lashes, then turned back to peer out the window.

Charles stalked quietly across the room and joined her at the window. She jumped when he whispered in her ear, "Thank you." She nodded but didn't turn around. He placed his hands around her hips and pulled her to him. "Shall we go and get dinner?"

"I'm not really hungry. I just want to remain here for the rest of the night. You can go ahead though."

"I'm not hungry for food," he said softly, feathering soft kisses along her neck. Elsa closed her eyes and savoured the feeling of his strong arms around her and his lips on the sensitive flesh just behind her ear. Her breathing quickened and she pressed into him, tilting her head to give him better access. He remained standing behind her and reached his hand down to the bottom of her blouse. He slowly pulled it upward until it was lifted over her head. Her shorts war removed next. She stood facing the window, clad in only her underwear. He reached around to cup her breasts as his planted kisses along her shoulders.

Charles caressed her torso until his hand right hand hovered at the waits of her panty. He slid his hand inside. Elsa gasped as his fingers brushed over her sensitive bud. "The light is on. What is someone sees us?"

He peered into the darkness, "I don't see anyone out there."

"But, there's no way you can see anything, it's too dark."

He could see perfectly fine with his advanced sight, but he couldn't mention it to reassure her. Instead, he swept her up and carried her to the huge bed. He laid her down gently and began to undress. Her eyes roamed over every inch of his toned body. Her gazed swung downward and her breath hitched as his erected shaft sprang free. Charles crawled onto the bed and stretched out beside.

Elsa sucked in a deep breath. *It's finally going to happen.* Excitement and a sliver of fear of the unknown went through her. "Open your legs," he commanded softly. She obeyed. He reached down to slip a finger inside of her, wringing a gasp from her lips. "You're ready," he whispered.

She licked her lips, "I am."

Charles positioned himself between her hips; his erection hovered at her entrance. He held her brown gaze as he slowly pushed forward. A strangled moan escaped her lips when he reached her barrier. "Hold on to me," he instructed. She wrapped her hands around his biceps. He surged forward in a swift movement. Elsa shrieked at the feel of a sharp pain and her nails dug into his skin; she shut her eyes tightly. The pain eased and the quickly became accustomed to the fullness of him inside her. Charles struggled to maintain his control, he wanted to thrust forward again, but held off on his own pleasure to slowly ease her into the process. "Are you ok?"

Elsa opened her eyes and met his gaze, she nodded. "Yes." He began to move inside of her with agonizingly slow, deep strokes. Elsa's eyes widened at the immense pleasure she now felt. She wrapped her legs around his waist, pulling him deeper. Charles let out a moan of pleasure as her tight sheath gripped him, like a well fitted glove.

"My God, Elsa you feel like heaven."

"More Charles," she whispered.

Startled, he glanced down at her. Her eyes were clouded with desire. He obliged and gave her what she asked for; he withdrew and plunged into her with more force. Elsa gasped the pleasure/pain coursing through her. His hips picked up speed and he plunged into her over and over, until she sobbed his name. The pleasure that course through Elsa as her orgasm hit her like a tidal wave cause her body to arch up off of the bed. "*Charles.*" As she moaned his name he too slipped over the edge into a sea of pleasure. He gritted his teeth to keep them from lengthening; and closed his eyes tightly so that Elsa didn't see his eyes change color. He dug his fingers into the sheets, willing his claws not to burst through. When he gained control over his wolf, he withdrew himself from inside her and collapse at her side.

Their ragged breaths mingled in the silence of the room. Elsa slowly floated back down to earth. "That was…mind blowing. I didn't know it could be like that," she whispered; glancing at him in wonder and amazement.

Charles gave a wide satisfied grin, extremely happy that he could make her first experience mind blowing, as she put it. "I'm glad you enjoyed it, so did I. You're amazing Elsa."

She smiled shyly her face flushed. She bit her lower lip and slowly lifted her gaze to his. "Um, can we go again right now?"

Charles gawked at her, and then let out a roar of laughter. He rolled her on top of him and held her to him, "I've created a monster." He captured her lips with his, kissing her intensely. "Of course we can go again, just give me a few minutes." She smiled down at him. She was glad she had waited to share her first sexual experience with such a man. It was like she had been saving herself for twenty-three years just for Charles. She gazed at him in wonder at the warmth that spread through her entire being. She rested her head on his chest, listening to the sound of his heart beat. Her fingers flew to her lips. *I love him.* Her eyes widened, she had only known Charles Grimm for a matter of days and she was in love with him. She had no idea what to do with that piece information. Should she tell him? *No.* She might scare him away; he would probably think it was too soon. Maybe he didn't feel the same way. It was best to keep her feelings to herself for now. She wished she could get some advice from Lisa right about now.

She shrieked in surprise when Charles suddenly flipped her over. She burst out giggled when she got over her initial shock. "You could have warned me."

"There's no fun in that," he murmured, nibbling on her ear. He wasted no time. He parted her thighs with his knee and slid into her softness. Elsa wrapped her arms around his neck and pulled him into a steaming kiss.

Charles lay with Elsa in his arms. He stared at the ceiling, waiting for Elsa to fall asleep. Her breathing slowed and deepened. He shifted to see if she would wake up. Satisfied when she didn't move, he cautiously untangled himself from her. He quickly dressed. Before he went through the door, he stopped to stare down at her. She looked so young and innocent with her hand curled under her chin. Her mass of auburn hair fanned out across the white pillowcase, like a vivid curtain. Her lips were curved into a slight smile. He was tempted to crawl back into bed with her. But, he couldn't; it was time to for him to go out and hunt. He had to find Victor and the mystery shifter. One or both of them had struck again. He needed to find them before another life was taken.

He made no sound as he padded along the hardwood floor, to the window. He pushed the window open and took one more look at Elsa. She was still fast asleep. His gaze swept the surrounding below and leapt out the window, landing agilely on his feet. He looked around again to make sure he had not been seen. He took off into a run, sprinting at super human speed into the heavily foliaged area. He kept running until he was hidden by a mass of trees. Stopping, he quickly undressed and hid his clothes under some plants. He stood up and transformed, his bones stretched the snapping audible. His face elongated into the shape of a wolf and his hands and feet spouted into lethal claws. He padded on large paws, sniffing the air. Victor was in the area. Of course the shifter would hide out in the wild. Any opportunity to run free in their wolf form was always ceased. Charles detected not scent of the other shifter. That was unfortunate; he would have loved to take out both opponents in one night.

He followed Victor's scent further into the wooded area. The fresh scent of fresh blood assailed his nostril, causing his mouth to water. He had not feed in a while. A cold feeling settled in the pit of his stomach. It seemed Victor had struck again, claiming another life. A low growl rumbled in his throat. He would rip the man apart; rid the world of him once and for all. The memory of Victor's attack on Elsa flashed in his mind, increasing his killing rage. He would never be a threat to her again.

Charles discovered Victor, crouched over a native woman's body. He whipped around when he smelled Charles. His eyes flashed and he took a step back. Charles's top lip retracted showing sharp, deadly fangs. He crouched low and leaped toward Victor, who quickly took his wolf form. He pounced meeting Charles in mid air. Both wolves hit the ground still entwined; claws clashed in the darkness. Victor's claws caught Charles across his face. He ignored the burning pain; he managed to avoid another blow. Charles held Victor down with powerful paws and bit down on his neck, his fangs sinking deep. Victor let out a howl, but stopped fighting. *Charles, listen to me. I'm not the enemy. I haven't killed anyone.* The words drifted in to Charles's mind. Startled, his head snapped up releasing Victor's neck, he took step back and cocked his head to head side. Victor had communicated with him telepathically as was their kind's way of communicating when in wolf form.

Like hell you didn't. What were you doing crouched over that woman's body?

Victor sighed, *I was not the one who killed that woman, or the two passengers on the ship.* Victor paused and looked into Charles's ferocious yellow eyes. *If you detected my scent, it was because I was there investigating, just like yourself. There was another shifter on the ship. He's good, cunning; he knows how to hide his presence well.*

Charles nodded inside his wolf, he agreed with Victor on that. He had not detected the other shifter's presence until he was right on top of him. *Who is he?*

I don't know. I have not seen the man before. I still don't know who he is, his face is always concealed.

Charles growled. *Forget about him for now. Let's talk about my father.*

I didn't kill your father. I found him already bleeding to death.

What the hell were you doing in his house then? Charles asked vehemently.

He had information that I wanted.

Information about what? Charles asked.

Victor hesitated, *Elsa Grey.*

Charles went completely still; he crouched ready to pounce on Victor again at the mention of Elsa's name. *What do you want with her?*

Relax; I don't want to hurt the girl. I want to protect her. She's my god daughter.

Charles was taken aback. *Your god daughter?*

Her father was my best friend. She has the shifter gene Charles. Her father was a shifter and her mother was human.

Charles let out a breath. He didn't know whether he should believe a word Victor said. *What do you feel the need to protect her from?*

Victor gave a snort; *well at first I thought I had to protect her from you. But, I realize you have been looking out for her the entire time.*

Charles frowned, *I would never hurt Elsa.*

Victor continued, *there is some of our kind who would seek to wipe out her existence. Fanatics who think that half breeds are an abomination to our kind. I have been following her for some time, watching over her. I promised her father I would look after her.*

Before Charles could question Victor any further, footsteps were heard approaching them. It appeared that some of the islanders were out searching for the woman who had gone missing. They would be in for a shock when they found her ravished body. Victor threw Charles a look, and they both took off in opposite directions. Charles's mind raced as he ran stealthily threw the woods. Elsa was half wolf. That explained his uncanny connection to her; even his wolf had felt the connection. He had received live changing information from Victor. He wondered if he could really trust the other shifter.

Chapter Five

Elsa stretched as she slowly came awake. She smiled feeling deliciously sore. Memories of her and Charles's vigorous love making the night before flashed across her mind. Just the mere memories aroused her. She reached over, feeling for him. Her hand landed on empty space. Her eyes opened and she sat up. She searched the room. Where was Charles? She glanced at the door; it was locked from the inside, so he had not gone through it. She felt a cool breeze and glanced over to the window. It was open. She was almost sure it had been locked last night.

A door pushed open and her head swung to her left. Charles emerged, a towel wrapped loosely around his waist. He was drying his wet hair with another. The bathroom, of course; why hadn't she thought of that? He flashed her grin. "Good morning beautiful."

She beamed competing with the sun light shining through the curtains. "Good morning." She admired the definition of his muscular body; her fingers itched to pull the towel from his waste and make love to him again. Oh no, she had become obsessed with having sex with Charles. He really had created a monster.

"Sleep ok?" He asked.

"Like a baby." She had been worn out and completely sated.

He smiled, "I'm glad to hear that. No more nightmares?"

She shook her head, "Not last night. My head was filled with thoughts of you." She blushed at her admission. Had she really just said that out loud?

Charles chuckled and dove onto the bed, rolling her beneath him. "I'm glad I could be of service." He kissed her briefly, and then lifted his head to study her intently.

Elsa frowned, "What?" She lifted her hand to self consciously at her tangled hair.

He shook his head, "It's nothing. Are you hungry? You didn't eat anything last night."

"I'm famished. I'm going to shower and get dressed. Elsa scooted from the bed and padded to the bathroom. The stood, letting the water beat down on her. She smiled slightly. Last night was incredible and it was even better waking up and having Charles with her. The circumstances of them being grounded on this island were unfortunate; but she now saw it as a blessing in disguise. The cruise ship was supposed to return to Miami in two days, and that would be the end of her vacation and her time with Charles. But now, she would get a little extra time to spend with the man she had fallen in love with. Their time together would eventually come to an end, but she will gladly take the few more days she would have with him All she had to do was make every moment count. When they parted ways, she would never forget him.

"Hey are you ok in there?" Charles called

"Uh, yes. I'm coming out now." She had spent a little longer than necessary in the shower because she had been lost in thought. A few minutes later, Elsa sauntered into the room wrapped in a towel. Charles was standing by the window, looking out. He turned when he hear her enter the room.

"Stop right there," Charles said softly. Confused she stopped in her tracks. "Drop the towel," he commanded huskily. *Oh.* Elsa quickly figured out where things were headed. Her pulse rate kicked up in anticipation. She released the towel and let it drop to the floor. "Walk to me, slowly." Elsa took slow steps toward him, stopping inches away. She looked up at him, waiting for his next command. He turned and pulled the window closed, then stepped aside. "Place your hand against the window." She did as she was told. He didn't touch her, simply studied her body as if ingraining every inch of her into his memory.

Charles stepped behind her and dropped his own towel. He stepped behind her and reached his hand around to stoke her clitoris. Elsa shuddered, her breath coming out in short puffs. "Bend over Elsa." She bent slightly at the waist, her hands still pressed against the window. Charles stepped back to admire her. Elsa nearly groaned out loud, Charles just studying her naked body and giving her orders was surprising erotic.

He finally stepped behind her and grabbed her hips; plunging into her tightness. "*Oh my*," Elsa breathed. She nearly came apart with one stroke. He moved behind her, reaching up to palm her small breasts. Charles taking her from behind was an entirely different sensation to her. She gazed out at the beauty of the tropical island. She knew that if anyone looked up and concentrated hard enough, they would see what was going on behind the closed window. The thrill of potentially being discovered turned her on even more.

"I can't get enough you Elsa," Charles whispered. Elsa couldn't speak; all she could do was moan. The pressure soon built within her core and exploded. Charles erupted simultaneously with her; shuddering his release. Elsa's knees buckled, weakened by an overload of pleasure. Charles steadied her, spinning her around to plant a hard kiss on her lips. "Are you alright?" He asked.

Elsa gazed up at him, still in a daze. "I-I'm *great*."

He grinned, "Good, now let's get out of here before we end up back in that bed."

"I wouldn't mind."

Charles laughed, "You need to eat. Get dressed." He gave her playful swat on the behind. She yelped and giggled, walking to her bag to find clothes. Charles smiled slightly. He turned back to gaze out the window. He still wasn't sure what to do with the information that Victor had given him. Could Elsa handle the truth? Or was it better to leave her in the dark? He shuddered at the thought that some of his kind wanted her dead. Maybe that was the mysterious shifter's motive. He had gone after her with intent to kill her. He ran a hand through his hair. What if the shifter had followed Elsa onto the Cruise ship? Could he somehow detect that she was half wolf?

"Aren't you going to get dressed?" Elsa asked, brining Charles out of his deep thoughts.

"Hmm? Oh, sure."

He quickly dressed and sat on the bed to wait for her. He studied her as she brushed her hair, humming a lively tune. Now more than ever he had to keep her in his sight. He now knew that she was a target. "You worry me sometimes, you know that?" He looked at her, confusion written on his handsome features. "You have this habit of just going silent. You stare into space as if you have entered another world or something." Elsa sighed; she wished he would let her in. She could probably help with whatever was bothering him, or at least just lend a listening ear. She was aware that he had no family left, just like her; and he was use to being alone. But, he didn't have to be, he had her. At least until they parted ways at the end of their vacation anyway.

"I'm sorry. It's just a bad habit. I think too much sometimes." She threw him an annoyed glance but remained silent. She finished getting putting herself together and turned to him.

"Ok, I'm ready." He stood up and reached for her hand. She smiled and placed her smaller hand in his large one.

"Elsa, Charles over here!" Tabitha waved them over to an outside table; Arnold smiled brightly at them. Elsa smiled and wave back. She and Charles walked over to the couple.

"Good morning, you two. How was your night?" Elsa asked.

Tabitha gushed, "It was lovely dear. I just love this island. It's so beautiful' it has a certain charm to it."

"It is lovely," Elsa agreed. She and Charles took the two empty seats at the table; and a waitress quickly approached. They ordered breakfast and returned their attention to the older couple.

Tabitha eyed them, "You two have been thick as thieves since you met. You don't see one without the other, isn't that right Arnie."

"That is true," Arnold agreed. "Reminds of us," he gazed at Tabitha lovingly.

Elsa smiled; it was so nice to see people still so much in love after so many years of marriage. She felt a pang of longing. That's what she wanted for herself. She glanced at Charles; she wouldn't mind having that that kind of life with him. But she knew it probably wouldn't happen, he wouldn't even confide in her. She sighed inwardly; they had not known one another for long. Maybe she was expecting too much. Or it was possible that he didn't think it was worth it to bring her too much into his life because their time together would soon end.

The waitress came back to their table with full trays. Elsa welcomed the distraction; anything to stop Tabitha and Arnold from delving deeper into the topic of her relationship with Charles. She quickly stuffed food into her mouth so that she wouldn't be expected to talk.

Arnold broke the silence, "So Charles, what is it that you do for a living son."

Tabitha glared at her husband, "Darling it's not polite to question the young folks about their business."

Arnold gave an innocent look, "Well, that's not too personal of a question. Is it?" He turned to Charles enquiringly.

He smiled slightly, not at all. "I buy companies, build them up and make them better; and then sell them to the highest bidder."

"Interesting, that takes a lot of business smarts son. You can make a killing off that kind of thing too."

Charles nodded, "I took over from my father."

Elsa sat silently; she had not even known what kind job he was into. Then it hit her, she really didn't know much at all about the man beside her. She only knew that she loved him. Of course, she didn't know anything about him; he was constantly hiding things from her. What was he hiding that was so bad, he couldn't tell her? She lost her appetite all of a sudden. "Um, Tabitha, Arnold; I'm not feeling so well all of a sudden. I think I need to lie down"

Tabitha gasped, "You poor thing, you do look a little pale. Shall I follow you to your room?"

"No it's ok, Stay and enjoy your breakfast." Elsa abruptly got up.

Tabitha studied her, concerned. "Maybe it's the heat that has you feeling ill."

"Yes, maybe." I will see you two later." Charles got rose from his seat to follow her. "No, you stay. I'm just going to go straight up to the room. I will be fine."

"I'm coming with. At least let me walk you up."

"I said I'm fine, there's no need. Finish your breakfast." Without waiting for him to respond she rushed off.

Elsa threw herself onto the bed. She didn't know why she was feeling so emotional. She let out a loud grunt; Charles had her feelings all in disarray, that's why. She rolled her eyes in annoyance. That didn't stop her from being in love with him. She felt guilty for lying about not feeling well. But she had just wanted to get away and be alone with her raging emotions for a little why. She felt like she was going to burst. She wished she could call Lisa and vent; but she hadn't seen Charles bring his cell phone. She wondered if she could find a computer with internet service anywhere. She got up to look out the window.

A figure moved quickly toward the foliage. Her gazed focused. *Charles?* She watched him as he glanced around, as if he was hiding. He held his nose up in the air. Was he smelling for something? Elsa's brows furrowed; that was strange. Why would he be sneaking and sniffing around? He walked further into the wooded area. She had to bend down to see him beneath the large trees. He was unbuttoning his shirt. *What in the world is he doing?* Elsa was alarmed by his strange behvior. Why in the world was Charles undressing on the bushed? Oh no, maybe he had some weird fetish. *Or maybe he's meeting someone else.* Elsa's heart shuddered at the thought. She wouldn't be surprised if it was the latter. He was after all and experience man of the world. He was seven years older that she was, maybe he was not satisfied with such a younger companion. Plus he was a billionaire; he could have any woman he wanted.

Elsa's shoulder sagged and tears sprung to her eyes. Just then, she saw someone else walking toward the same direction Charles had gone in. She took a closer look. Elsa gasped, *Mr. Creepy*. Oh no, what if he had seen Charles enter the woods alone and he followed to do him some kind of harm. She had to make sure Charles was ok; or at least warn him. She tuned and dashed to the door. She quickly made it outside and ran into the woods where the two men had gone.

She rand until her lungs burned. She saw no sight of them. She stopped to breath, placing her palms on her knees. They must be moving super fast, she should have caught if they were still walking. She straightened to start running again, but glimpsed movement in the distance. She hid behind a tree and peeked around to see who or what it was. Her eyes widened in shock.

The animal before her was no ordinary wildlife; it was massive black wolf. *Holy crap,* there was no way a normal wolf grew to that size; she at least knew that much. The thing was almost taller than she was. Did wolves even live in tropical regions? The wolf's head turned in her direction, sniffing the air as if it had detected something; its yellow eyes scanning its surroundings. She disappeared behind the tree trunk and held her breath, careful not to make a sound. The wolf's eyes were the same yellow as the shadowy creature that plagued her in her dreams; and the same color she thought she had seen flash in Mr. Creepy's eyes. But that was just not possible.

She waited a few heartbeats then slowly peeked around the tree again. The abnormally large wolf had sauntered of. Caroline was beyond intrigued by the mutation of nature and couldn't help but trail the animal. She followed it, but lost sight of the animal. It sure moved fast for such a massive creature. At this point, she wanted to turn around and high tail it back to the hotel. But, Charles was out here somewhere and he not only was Mr. Creepy stalking him, but a ferocious wild animal was out here. She stopped suddenly; the two people who had been murdered on the ship seemed as if they had been attacked by a wild animal. Could the wolf she saw now have somehow been on board? Maybe it had been hidden in the lower most part of the ship. She shook her head; it was almost impossible for such an imposing creature to go undetected on a *cruise* ship.

She walked further. A man strolled out into the clearing and she almost called out to warn the man about the large predator. But she remained silent; the animal was nowhere to be seen. The man looked familiar; she was sure she had seen him a few times on the ship. She frowned as the man began to strip naked. *What the hell?* Why was everyone undressing for goodness sake? When the man was completely naked, he rolled his head from side to side. Elsa almost fainted when she saw his face elongate into the shape of a wolf. His body stretched and deadly looking claws replaced human hands. Within seconds a giant gray wolf stood in the man's place. She gasped, her hands flying to cover her mouth. The animal's head came up sharply, it yellow gazing landing directly on her. *Oh no.* It growled and took off toward her in long strides. She scrambled backward and took off into a run. She knew she would never be able to out run the animal. She screamed, hoping that someone would hear her.

Charles sat in his wolf form, hidden in the bushed. He was waiting for Victor. He stayed on high alert. He still wasn't sure if he could trust the other shifter. A blood curdling scream sounded nearby. His head whipped up. He knew that scream. *Elsa?* It couldn't be she was supposed to be in their room resting. He sniffed the air; her familiar scent assailing is olfactory sense. *Elsa.* He sprinted off, whizzing past trees at a paranormal. The ground shook beneath his massive paws with each step.

He heard her scream again, the gut wrenching sound laced with absolute terror. Panic rose up in him as he followed her voice and her scent. He jumped in to a clearing, terrified at the scene playing out before him. Elsa stumbled back, hitting the ground with loud thud. She crawled backward as a black wolf loomed over her, his sharp teeth bared, ready to attack. Charles let out a growl and lunged toward the other wolf, hitting him square in the chest. It clawed at him, making a long, deep jagged slash across Charles's chest. The black wolf fell on its back and sprung agilely to its feet. Charles placed himself between Elsa and the wolf.

Before the wolf could pounce again, gray wolf leapt out of the foliage, and grabbed the black wolf around its neck with sharp teeth. It was victor. The injured wolf managed to break free and sprint off. Victor tuned to Charles and nodded, indicating that he would take care of the other shifter. Charles turned to Elsa who was backing away. Her eyes were wide and her breaths were coming out in rapid puffs. She looked dazed and deathly pale. She screamed again as he approached her. He did the only thing he could to let her know he wasn't going to hurt her; he transformed back into his human self. "Elsa, it's me." She made a weird, strangled sound and her eyes rolled back. Her head hit the ground with a thud, and she laid deathly still.

Chapter Six

"*Elsa!*" Charles rushed to kneel beside her. He felt her pulse, thankful that she was still breathing; she had just fainted.

He ran a hand over his face, thinking quickly. He remembered that is clothes were stashed nearby and ran to get them. He speedily donned his garments and moved back to Elsa, scooping her up off the ground. He had to get her out of here. He looked back, wondering if Victor was alright to handle the other shifter by himself. It would seem the man was telling the truth. He really had been protecting Elsa. He just put himself at risk to help save her. He could only hope Victor could hold his own with the other wolf. He moved through the wooded area at a great speed. He reached the clearing in record time and the hotel came into view.

He glanced around to see if anyone was watching. He ran to a back entrance and thankfully made it to the room undetected. He laid Elsa down on the bed. She still showed no sign of waking up. He ran his fingers through his hair. He was really starting to worry. Why was she so pale? He sat beside her and tapped her jaw. "Elsa, please wake up." He tapped a little harder when he received no response. He lashes finally fluttered and her eyelids slowly lifted. She looked confused and her eyes were unfocused. She groaned, lifting her hand to rub the back of her head. There was developing bump. She winced at the tenderness at the area.

Her gaze shifted to him, "Charles? What happened?"

He stared down at her. "You fainted."

"I did? How embarrassing? Did I see blood or something?" She always got a little woozy when she saw blood.

"Um, no." He had no idea what to tell her. She didn't seem to remembering anything about him transforming from animal to human before her eyes. Maybe it was for the best. She stared up at him and frowned. She looked away and burst out into a fit of laughter. She stopped to hold her head, wincing in pain; but continued to smirk. *Oh no, she's hysterical.* He had no idea what to do when someone was hysterical.

"I had the strangest dream. It was about giant wolves." Charles's eyebrows shot up but he remained silent. What was there to say? "It seemed so real." She stopped talking for a few moments as she contemplated something.

Charles watched her closely. Her eyes widened. "That's because it was real." She looked at Charles, waiting for him to tell her that it had to be a dream. But he said nothing, just stared at her guiltily. She shot up off of the bed and scooted away from him. Why wasn't he denying her statement? A sick feeling washed over her and she thought she might faint again. *No, no, no.* There was no way she had seen Charles transform from giant brown wolf. She also remembered seeing a strange man turn into a black wolf; and then a gray wolf had come out of nowhere. Those things only happened in movies. It couldn't be real. Either Charles was playing a very sick joke on her or she was losing her mind. It had to be the latter. Yes, she was going insane. She was having hallucinations about giant wolves tuning into people and people turning into wolves. The heat of the island had probably gotten to her.

Charles looked down at his hands and back up at her, his expression pained. "Elsa..." He shook his head. He didn't know what to say. He blew out a breath. "Everything that you witnessed was real. She got up off the bed, shaking her head.

"But how? I-I don't understand." She searched her memories. Things started to come back to her. Mr. Creepy's eyes flashing yellow; Charles sniffing the air and undressing as he snuck into the woods. The night when they were attacked she had seen the masked man throw Charles across the deck with one hand. Charles wasn't a small man. That same night she could have sworn she heard Charles give an almost animalistic growl. She dug deeper. The memory of the wound on his shoulder flashed through her mind. She realized that she had not even see scar. It was not humanly possible for the scar to disappear so fast. Elsa grabbed her head with both hands. Her head was starting to pound.

Oh my God. That was how the animal that killed the two passengers had gotten on board in the first place. She gasped, clutching her chest. Had Charles been responsible for any of the murders? She threw him a suspicious glance. Elsa swayed on her feet. Charles rushed toward her. "Don't come near me!"

Startled, he drew back. "Please sit before you fall Elsa."

"Don't tell me what to do. There is no way I'm staying in here with-with a-a..."

"Wolf shifter," he finished.

Elsa groaned, "Oh God, really?" She threw her hand up in the air. He didn't even try to deny it. "Did you have anything to do with the murders on the ship?"

"What? Of course not. I don't make a habit of killing humans." Elsa let out a relieved breath. Well at least he wasn't a murderer. Not that she knew of anyway.

Charles took a step toward her. She turned and made a dash for the door. Before she could get it fully open, he was behind her pushing the door closed with one hand. Elsa whipped around, shrinking against the door. She closed her eyes tightly, "Please don't eat me."

"I'm not going to eat you."

She opened one eye and peeked up at him. Charles lifted a hand to caress her cheek. When she flinched, he dropped his hand to his side. "You don't have to be afraid of me Elsa; I'm not going to hurt you."

"Well excuse me for being cautious. You're wolf friend did try to eat me."

"He is not my friend; I have no idea who he is." She looked unconvinced. "If I wanted to hurt you, don't you think I would have already? Think of how many opportunities I've had. He lowered his head to hers. What about last night when I had you pinned beneath me? What about when I entered you and you had your eyes closed?" His lips moved dangerously close to hers. Her breath hitch and her tongue darted out to moist her lip. "What about when you fell asleep in my arms? Or when you were pressed against the window and I took from behind this morning?" His lips hovered hover hers. Her eyes fluttered closed and she waited, anticipated the touch of lips to hers. He abruptly pulled away. "Don't you think I could have hurt you then; or even now?

Elsa remained silent, leaning against the door for support. She cursed her traitorous body for responding to him, when she was afraid him. She swallowed and nodded, "Ok, point well made and taken." She slowly stepped away from the door. He was right, he'd had plenty of time to do her harm if he had intended. He had also saved her life on several occasions. If he had wanted her dead, he would have let her fall to her death that night when she hung precariously from the ledge.

He turned to her, sadness seeping through his very pores. "Now you see what I have been hiding from you Elsa. You begged me to tell, but I knew you weren't ready. I knew you would react exactly like you are now." He wiped a hand over his face, "Look at you, you're terrified of me; and I would rather stab myself in the heart with a silver dagger than lift a hand to hurt you."

Elsa blinked. Holy crap; so the thing about silver killing wolves was true. She shook her head; this was all too much for her take in. It was just her luck that the man she had fallen in love with was some kind of shape shifter. No wonder she was so attracted to him. She was terrible at connecting with humans, but had no problem connecting with him. Now she knew why- he wasn't human. She dropped her head in her hands. What was she going to do now? Run for the hills? Report him to the authorities? She sighed; she could never give him up. The thought of what they would do to him was terrifying. That proved that despite what she had just found out, she still loved him.

Charles sank onto the bed. He felt defeated. He was about to lose Elsa for sure; because of his dark secret. His dropped and his shoulders drooped. What was he expecting? That she was going accept what he was and run off into the sunset with him. He grunted, he should have been prepared for this. He was about to lose the most important thing in his life, because of what he was.

The utter sadness and defeat radiating from Charles, tugged at Elsa's heart strings. What was the matter with her? She was the one who had gotten angry with him for hiding things from her. Now she was finally getting the truth out of him and she couldn't accept it. She sighed, Charles was an amazing person. She should at least try to give him a chance. "So you're a werewolf? There was no full moon; it was broad daylight."

He lifted his head in surprise, "Uh, no. Wolf shifters are different from werewolves. We can shift between human and wolf voluntarily, on impulse without a full moon."

"Ok so you pretty much just made it clear that werewolves are indeed real. Wow, how am I going to take all of this in." Charles watched in utter chock as Elsa walked toward him, stopping in front of him. She placed her fingertips under his chin and gently lifted his face. He held her gaze. "Do your eyes turn yellow too?" He gave her a demonstration; his hazel eyes flashed a bright yellow. Elsa sucked in a breath, her fingers moved from his chin to caress his jaw. "Does it hurt when you... shift?"

A sheen of tears glistened in his eyes. She wasn't running; she was touching him. Asking him questions about what he was, like she was ready to accept him. He swallowed hard and placed his hand over hers as she stroked his face. "It does the stretching of my bones hurt every time."

She frowned, she didn't like that he experience pain. She eased her way between his legs and sat on his lap. He gasped, when she wrapped her hands loosely around his neck and gazed into his eyes. "What else can you do?"

His lips curved into a smile, "I'm super fast and strong. I have accelerated healing."

She glanced at him, "I'm a bit confused. Are you human too?"

He shrugged, "I guess you can say I'm both human and wolf."

"C-can you die?" She asked in a small voice.

"Wolf-shifters are immortal, due to our increased healing. We are also immune to all conventional illnesses, viruses, diseases, and infections. But there are ways that we can be killed."

"With silver bullets?"

He nodded, "Silver is deadly to us."

She took a deep breath. "I'm sure there is more to tell and I definitely have a lot of questions, but I don't think I can digest anymore right now."

Charles nodded, "I understand." That meant he couldn't bring up the fact that her father was a wolf shifter too; or anything about Victor. He would ease everything else in slowly. "He reached up and pushed a lock of hair behind her ear. "You're an amazing woman Elsa, I'm lucky to have met you." She inched closer to him until their lips met. He lips moved hesitantly at first, the thought of him sprouting fangs flashed across her mind. He held back, allowing her full control. She gradually, began to move her lips more vigorously against his. She held his face between both hands and pushed her tongue into the warmness of his mouth.

Elsa broke the kiss abruptly, "Wait what about the other wolves that I saw?"

"I have no idea where they went."

"So you guys aren't travelling together?"

"I told you, I've never met them before?"

"One of them is definitely the murderer; or maybe even both of them."

Charles groaned, "Elsa please don't get any ideas, stay out of it. I don't want you getting hurt."

She threw him an annoyed glance, "Fine." She got up and moved away from him. She shook her head, "All of this so crazy. I still don't know this is real or if I'm dreaming."

"It's real. I'm real and what we have between us is real."

"What exactly is this thing between us Charles?" She knew that she loved him. But did he feel the same for her? Was he thinking about a life with her beyond this vacation, like she was?"

"Elsa I- A scream from outside stopped his response. Elsa ran to the window, Charles close behind. A crowd was forming below.

"I wonder what has happened this time," Elsa muttered.

Charles sighed; couldn't they have just one moment of peace? "Stay here, I'm going to find out what is going on."

"I'm going."

He gave her a stern look, "*Elsa.*" Now that he knew there were definitely people after her, he felt uneasy about her standing in a crowd, she would be too vulnerable. She crossed her arms and glared at him defiantly. He gave in "Fine, but stay close to me."

"Ok, I will." She followed him out the door.

As they approached the crowd, the smell of blood permeated the air. Elsa immediately felt ill. Not again. "You were right, I should have stayed inside," she muttered. A lifeless body was sprawled in the bushes; his chest cavity was ripped wide open. "Oh my God," Elsa turned for the macabre sight burying her face in Charles's chest. He held on to her and made no move to go any closer. He didn't need to he already knew how the man had died. The unknown shifter had struck again. Either he had done this before their confrontation in the woods or Victor had failed in killing him. That would mean that Victor was most likely dead. *Damn it,* he was getting to like the idea of having another shifter on his side. It made life much easier.

Charles glanced down at the sound of Elsa's gasp. She had turned around to peep at the body. "Isn't that the captain?"

"Charles took another look, "I'll be damned, it is."

A middle aged, balding man stepped out and turned to the crowd. "Hear me, all of you good people. I know who had been committing these heinous killings; or rather, I know *what*." There was a ripple among the crowd as they gave the man their full attention.

Someone shouted out, "If you know who, let the authorities know, so they can put the bastard behind bars." The crowd murmured in agreement."

"You fool, if the authority had any deal how to deal with this, the killer would be caught already. A human is not responsible for this, an abomination of nature is. There is a shape shifter among us!"

Charles stiffened and Elsa drew in a sharp breath. The man continued, "I have been tracking the abomination since we boarded the ship. I wasn't sure one was actually present until the killings started."

Someone in the crowd roared "Get out of here you crazy old man! There is no such thing as a shape shifter." The crowed agreed and turned to glare at the man.

He flushed a bright red, "You idiots don't know the half of what is going on in this world. By all means, keep your heads stuck in the sand

Chapter Seven

Charles stiffened and Elsa drew in a sharp breath at the man's words. She glanced up at Charles questioningly. Did other people know about the existence of his kind? The look on his face told her that humans were not supposed to know the secret. *Well the cat is out of the bag*, she thought; or rather the wolf was out of the bag.

The man continued, "I have been tracking the abomination since we boarded the ship. I wasn't sure one was actually present until the killings started."

Someone in the crowd roared "Get out of here you crazy old man! There is no such thing as a shape shifter." The crowed agreed and turned to glare at the man.

He flushed a bright red, "You idiots don't know the half of what is going on in this world. By all means, keep your heads stuck in the sand. Turn a blind eye. You shall all perish!" Everyone tuned to walk away from the man, throwing him annoyed looks.

"That man sounds crazy and *dangerous*," Elsa whispered as they followed the crowd.

"Another fanatic. As long as we have existed, there have been a selected group of men and women who consider themselves warriors of Christ. They seek to destroy everything non-human. I am ashamed to say, we have made things bad for ourselves; if some of us didn't go around killing people just for the fun of it, our existence would never have been discovered."

Elsa tightened her grip on Charles, "You have to stay away from him." She gazed up at him with fear in her eyes.

He grinned down at her, "I'm glad to see that you are still concerned about me."

"Of course I am," she hissed. "I love- I don't want anything to happen to you."

"I'll be fine," Charles whispered, leaning down to kiss her. "I have something I want to show." He led her in to the foliage.

"Where are we going?"

"It's surprise." Charles didn't want to risk taking Elsa out of the safety of the hotel. But he figured he would quickly take her to what he had discovered, and take her back to their room. She followed him, laughing at hi obvious excitement. They walked for quite a while going deeper and deeper into the wooded area. What could he possibly have to show her all the way out here? She giggled when he stopped and covered her eyes with her hand. "Ok watch your step."

She cautiously stepped forward, "Charles what is it? Show me already?" He removed his hand from her eyes. She blinked. Her eyes widened with pleasure, she gasped. "Wow. Charles this is absolutely beautiful," she breathed. Before her was waterfall, cascading into a small pool of clear pristine water beneath. The area was surrounded by low colourful foliage. "When did you discover this?"

"The first night we docked here."

She looked at him confused, "But you were with me all night."

He gave her a sheepish grin, "I snuck out after you fell asleep, to hunt down the other shifters."

She glowered at him, "I didn't hear the door open."

"I didn't use the door."

Her eyes widened, so that's why she had woken up to find the window open. He had jumped all the way from the sixth floor? "The window huh? I'm impressed."

Charles grinned like a school boy, proud that he had impressed the pretty girl. "Ok, time to go back."

"And leave this spectacular view? Can't we stay a bit?"

"It's getting dark."

She grinned seductively at him and turned to wind her arms around his neck. "The darker the better." She stood on the tip of her toes to reach his lips.

"Charles groaned, "You little minx. Ok we can stay for five more minutes."

"That's all we need." She turned and stripped naked. She then tuned to walk to the waterfall, beckoning him to follow. He watched the sway of her naked bottom, hypnotized by the movement. He stripped his clothes off as he followed behind her, his shaft hardening in anticipation. She stepped behind the curtain o water. "Come here," she said softly. He did as he was told. She pushed him gently against a flat rock and bent down, her face now level with his erection. She gazed up at him through her lashes and smiled seductively. His breath hitched when he realized what she intended to do.

"Elsa you don't have to."

She ignored him and took his erection into her hands, stroking gently. She slowly covered the tip with her mouth and he moaned. She took him deeper into her mouth, moving her head slowly. Charles gritted his teeth and threw his head back. He reached down to tangle his fingers in her hair. Her back and forth movement was driving him mad. If she didn't stop, he would explode into her mouth. "Elsa, you have to stop." He gently pulled her to her feet, planting passionate kiss on her lips. He lifted her to him and she wrapped her legs around his waist. He slowly bought her down on his shaft until he filled her completely.

Elsa wrapped her arms around his neck, breathing rapidly. He lifted her hips and bought her back down, wringing a soft moan from her lips. He began to move his hip faster, bringing them both to the brink of ecstasy. They soon exploded together. Elsa clung to him, her body still wrapped around his. "We should go," he whispered into her ear."

"Ok" she agreed.

He slowly put her down. Her knees felt weak when her feet touch the ground. Charles always had that effect on her; made her weak in the knees. They located their clothes and quickly dressed. Elsa gave him one more kiss before they walked off toward the hotel. It was dark by then and Charles had to guide her through the foliage. "We have to come back here before we leave. It's so gorgeous and quiet. I could hang out here all day."

He smiled, glad that she was pleased with his surprise. He knew she would absolutely love it. When he had stumbled up on the area, he had immediately thought of her. The water fall and pool was almost as beautiful as she was. He had not imagined that she would end up seducing him under the waterfall. He was glad that he had decided to take her there tonight. It was an experience he would remember for a life time. "So I guess we are going to pick up where we left off when we get back to our room."

Charles chuckled, "You are wearing me out Ms. Grey; you're insatiable." He pulled her in for a peck on the cheek. "I love it." He was about to tell her that he also loved *her*. But a small noise in the distance interrupted him. It sounded like someone has stepped on a twig. He sniffed the air. It was a human. What was anyone doing out in this area at night? Unless they were doing what he and Elsa had just been engaged in. As the person got closer, Charles's lips pulled back into a snarl. He released a menacing growl. It was the fanatic who had been preaching about shifters earlier. He couldn't be up to anything good. Charles gently pushed Elsa behind him.

"Hold it right there," the man snarled. He pointed a gun straight a Charles's heart. "This gun is loaded with silver bullets; move and you die demon."

Charles stared at the man with deadly intensity. He vowed to rip the man's throat out. Elsa gasped behind him. "No, please put your weapon down," she stepped out.

"Elsa get back," Charles growled.

"He's going to kill you," she hissed.

The man's eyes flew to Elsa, "What are you planning to do to that poor girl? Were you going to make her you next meal?"

Elsa rolled her eyes, "No, he would never hurt me. He's my boyfriend. So please just put the gun down and let us pass."

"What are you doing with this abomination? You do understand that he is a monster? You are just as disgusting as he is. You deserve to be punished for fornicating with *it*."

"I have no idea what kind of abomination you speak of sir. He is my boyfriend and nothing more," Elsa said.

He shifted the gun to Elsa, "Come with me now."

"She is not going anywhere with you," Charles hissed.

The man tuned to Elsa, "If you don't come with me, I will kill him," he pointed the gun back at Charles.

Elsa gasped, "No please don't. I'll go with you, just let him go."

"Elsa stand back," Charles said. He would be damned if he let Elsa leave with that insane man. He rushed forward to wipe out the threat to Elsa. The man pulled the trigger and a shot rang out.

Elsa let out a scream, "Charles no!" Charles fell to his knees. He saw the man grab Elsa and dragged her away. She clawed and kicked at him, trying to make her way back to him. "Charles!" The man used the butt of his gun to knock her unconscious. She hit the ground with a thud and he picked her up and threw her over his shoulder.

Charles watches as they disappeared into the darkness. Elsa hung lifelessly on her captor's shoulder. "Elsa," Charles whispered. She had been taken from him and he couldn't move to help her. He had to get her out of the mad man's clutches; there was no telling what he was going to do to her. She would also be vulnerable to the other shifter who sought to kill her. Charles staggered to his feet, blood poured from him, making him to weak. He took a few short steps, determined to follow the man and get the love of his life back in his arms. He dropped to his knees as his vision blurred. He slumped down to the ground. *Elsa.*

Deadly Secrets
Part 3: The Fight for Love

Chapter One

Charles lay on the ground, surrounded by thick green foliage. The sounds of the night echoed in the darkness. The trees swayed gently in the soft tropical breeze; and the leaves and plants on the ground rustles as critters passed over them. The crash of the ocean could be heard hitting against the rocks nearby. With his enhanced hearing, Charles could hear the receding footsteps of the man who had wounded him and kidnapped Elsa. He wondered where the man was taking her. It was a small island, so it could not be anywhere too far. Pain rippled through his body like a tidal wave. He tried to breath; but each breath he took bought on a fresh wave of pain. He let out a low groan, clenching his jaw. The thought of Elsa and his need to get to her; to rescue her from the clutches of that mad man was all that kept him struggling and holding to life. He was getting closer and closer to slipping into the darkness. *No.* He refused to succumb to it. He had to save Elsa. He had to get his love back into his arms. Images of her vivid auburn hair and innocent brow eyes flashed through his mind. Memories of the times they have shared in the few days they have been on the cruise ship and this island played across his mind.

His lips curved into a faint smile. He was so weak from blood loss that it took great effort just to lift the corners of his mouth into the smile. His hand flew to the wound on the left side of his abdomen. It was a good thing the man who had shot him had poor aim. The silver bullet had missed his heart by a mile. But, silver was lethal to his kind; and the bullet near his side was still doing serious damage. It weakened him immensely. His kind had accelerated healing, but his wound was not going to heal with the silver bullet still lodged inside of him. If it was not a silver bullet, his body would have pushed it out and begin to heal itself already. But that was not about to happen. He needed to get the bullet out somehow.

He pulled his hand away from his wound; it came away soaked with blood. He mustered all the strength he could and pulled himself to slump against the trunk of a tree. Just then, he heard soft footsteps in the distance. He stiffened; *damn it*. He was not in any condition to take on any threat at the moment. If that was one of his enemies; they could easily overpower and kill him. Charles grunted, he wondered if it was the same mad man that had put the bullet in him. Maybe he was coming to finish off the job he had started.

Charles released a string of curses in to the silence. He swung his head around weakly. He had to conceal himself and hope that whoever was approaching would not detect his presence. He spotted a thick cluster of bushes a few feet saw. He sighed, wondering if he could make the distance. He had to try. He used his hand to pull himself across to the bushes. He collapsed on to his back. It was hopeless, he was much too weak and his remaining strength was quickly dwindling. He stopped moving and stared up at the night sky the moon shone brightly and the stars twinkled. His breathing slowed ad his eyes fluttered downward. He felt like he could not hold on any long. *I'm so sorry Elsa.* His heart fluttered, he had failed her. He had failed to protect her and he would now fail to rescue from the hands of a mad man. There was no telling what he would do to her; what she would suffer at his hands.

The foliage parted and someone emerged. Charles caught a whiff the person's scent. Victor? The man rushed toward him. Charles opened his eyes. Victor loomed over him, concern written across his features. Charles grinned slightly, "Victor, I will be damned. You are still alive."

Victor cocked an eyebrow, "Of course I am; which is more than I can say for you. You look like you are knocking on death's door my friend."

Charles snorted rudely, "Friend? Since when are we friends?"

"You had better be more polite. As I see it, I am the one standing between you and certain death right now."

Charles chuckled, "Alright then, *friend*."

Victor shot him a sardonic smile. "I'm going to have to dig that bullet out of you."

"Charles shrugged, "Go ahead, and have at it." He steeled himself in preparation for the agony that was about to ensue. Victor knelt beside him and assisted Charles into a flat, supine position. He wasted no time reaching his finger into the small bullet hole. Charles grunted in pain and ground his teeth in an effort not to shout out in an expression of his pain. "Damn it, Victor. Take it easy will you?"

"Hush up, you big baby." He swirled his finger around. "Ah, I've got it," he said as his finger touched the small piece of metal. He slowly pulled it out of the tiny hole that was made in Charles's abdomen.

Charles groaned, "Why do I get the feeling that you enjoyed that way too much?"

Victor grinned wickedly, "No comment." He held the silver bullet between his thumb and index finger, studying it. "How can such a tiny thing do us so much damage?" He flicked the bullet away as if it had burned his fingers. "Well, you can go ahead and heal yourself now."

Charles studied Victor intently. He had been unsure about trusting the man before; but it seemed as if he could. If the man was really an enemy he could have easily killed Charles in his weakened, vulnerable state. "Thank you, Victor. I guess I owe you one."

Victor nodded, "No, I would say we are even. After all, you have been protecting Elsa this whole time." Charles sighed. Elsa, Victor's god daughter and the love of his life; just the sound of her name kicked his pulse into overdrive. He had to get her back.

Charles glanced at Victor guiltily, "I did not do such a good job protecting her tonight. She was taken."

"Yes, and I am very upset that you let that happen. But, don't beat yourself up over it. There isn't much you could have done with a silver bullet lodged inside of you. By the way, you are a lucky bastard; if whoever shot you was more skilled, the bullet could have gone through your heart."

"Don't remind me," Charles muttered. It might as well have gone through his heart, if he did not get Elsa back. "I need to find Elsa." He attempted to push himself up off the ground.

Victor pushed him back down with one hand. "Relax; you are not in any position to go on any rescue mission tonight." Victor peered down at him, "What the hell were you two doing out here this time of night anyway?"

Erotic images of Elsa kneeling naked before him, slowly taking his length into her mouth; and then him lifting her onto him, flashed through his mind. Charles threw the older man a sheepish look, "Uh well... we were... exploring."

Victor frowned, "Exploring what?" Then understanding dawned on him. He shook his head as if trying to get rid of the images now planted in his mind. He held his hand up, "You know what, never mind. Don't answer, I really don't need to know." He glanced down at Charles and growled, "Couldn't you two have done *that* in your damn hotel room?"

Charles sat up, his strength already returning. He ran his fingers through his hair, "I know it was less than smart of me to bring her out here." Charles hung his head as guilt washed over him. He had carried Elsa out into the wooded area to surprise her with what he had discovered. He knew she would love the scenery; since she had expressed wanting to explore the island. He had been right; he had watched in satisfaction as she gushed over the beauty of the waterfall and its surroundings. His heart had swelled with the knowledge that he was responsible for her excitement and the huge smile on her face.

After the traumatizing way she had found out that he was a wolf shifter, he wanted to lighten the mood. The memory of her terror when she had witness him shift from wolf to human before her eyes came back to him. His lifted his gaze to Victor, "I just wanted to make her happy. But all I did was put her in danger. I deserved to be shot with a silver bullet for that." He closed his eye, a deep feeling of regret taking over him.

Victor stared at Charles intently, his blue eyes roaming over the younger man's miserable expression. "You are in love with her?"

Startled, Charles's eyes flew open. He drew in a deep breath and nodded, "Somewhere along the way it happened. I tried to stay away from her, for her own safety. I didn't want to drag her into my dangerous world. But, our pull to each other was too much for either of us to resist." He sighed, "I vowed to protect her and I failed."

Victor remained silent for a moment, just thinking. "It would seem Elsa is your true life mate."

Charles frowned, "That is what I was thinking but, she is human."

"A human with the shifter gene; don't forget, her father was a shifter." Victor threw his hands up, "I spend years watching over her from the background, trying to keep her from the likes of you; and what happens? She ends up right in your bloody arms. I am the one who has failed. I have failed her and her father." He shook his head, "I am getting way too old for this."

Charles glared daggers at Victor, "What do you mean the likes of *me*? You are a damn wolf shifter too." Charles was finally able to stand on his feet. "Let us stop wasting time and find her already."

Victor stood up to face him, "Look at you, you can barely stand. You are not going anywhere; you will easily be killed. I will go and rescue her." He stopped speaking abruptly, and then glanced at Charles.

"Why are you looking at me like that?" Charles suddenly became alarmed. "What is it?"

"The other shifter, the one that tried to kill Elsa, he is still alive. He will have easy access to her without our protection."

Charles groaned, "I thought you took care of him."

"I barely escaped with my life. The shifter is strong and cunning. He got away."

Charles's shoulders sagged. He was tired and weak. "That means you can't go looking for Elsa alone. We now have a strong wolf shifter *and* an insane fanatic to worry about. You might very well be killed before you can rescue her. It is going to take the both of us."

"In your weakened state, even if the both of work together, we will still be killed." He gave Charles a pitying glance, "No offense, but you are completely useless at the moment my friend."

Charles grudging agreed, "You are right. I need to be at full strength."

Victor nodded, "What I will do is locate where the man has taken Elsa. I will stay out of sight. Then when you are strong enough we will get her back."

"Sounds like a plan." Charles stopped Victor before he took off, "Oh, Victor one more thing. She knows."

Victor's eyebrows shot up, "What are you talking about?"

"She knows about us; about wolf shifters."

Victor threw his hands up and sighed, "Why the hell would you tell her about our existence. She would have been better off if she didn't know."

"It was kind of hard not to tell her the entire truth after she saw us with her own two eyes. Don't you remember?" Elsa had been attacked by the unknown shifter; and both Charles and Victor had stepped in to save her.

"What she saw were three wolves and nothing more. That could have been explained."

"Uh, yes but then I shifted in front of her." Charles sent Victor a guilty look.

Victor glowered at him, "I am starting to regret saving your life. Why in the hell would you do something so stupid?"

"She deserved to know the truth. She knew that I was hiding the truth from her and she was hurt by it. I hated lying to her Victor. Relax;

she doesn't know anything about you. As far she knows, you're just a creepy stalker."

"What did you just say?" Victor's gaze flew to his, his brows furrowing.

"Uh, nothing. That is another story for another time."

Victor hesitated, wondering what Charles was talking about. He shook his head, then took off into the bushes. Whatever that vague comment was about was not that important at the moment."

Charles watched Victor run off. He leaned against the huge tree. He needed to get back to the hotel. He didn't like the idea of resting while Elsa was still in the grasp of a mad man. But, he was no good to her in his present state. He needed to be at full strength when he went for. He had a feeling he would have to fight like hell to get her back. The man who had shot him and took her from him was a religious fanatic and it seemed he was treading the path of insanity; that was a very dangerous combination. There was also the unknown shifter, who Charles was sure would make another attempt to get rid of Elsa. He needed to be fully recovered before he went on a rescue mission. He willed her to be strond until he could get to her.

Chapter Two

Elsa came awake slowly. Her lashes fluttered as she opened her eyes. *Ouch.* It felt like someone had beaten her over the head with an iron bat. She groaned, lifting her hand to rub the sore area on her head; but her hand went no further. Something heavy restricted her movement. Confused, she looked down; her hands were chained. Alarm shot through her and she became fully awake. Her eyes flew open and she sat up, ignoring the pain that shot through her head. She took in her surroundings. She was on a hard, cold concrete floor; in a dark and dank room. Why was she chained to the floor?

Then, her memories came flooding back. She and Charles were walking back to the hotel after an episode of erotic love making under a waterfall. She smiled slightly at the memory; but the smile was quickly wiped from her face as everything else came back. They were confronted by the crazy man who had been spouting nonsense about shape shifters and abominations, earlier that day, when another body had been discovered. The ravaged body looked like a n animal attack; much like the murders that had taken place before. Elsa gasped; she remembered a gun pointed at Charles and then her. The crazy man had demanded that Elsa leave with him or he would kill Charles. Of course, she had agreed; she didn't want se Charles get shot. She knew the silver bullet could kill him.

Charles had rushed forward to attack the gun wielding mad man. A shot had sounded in the night. The last thing Elsa remembered was Charles dropping to his knees, as she was dragged away. She closed her eyes tightly and shook her head from side to side. *No, no, no; he can't be dead. He can't be.* The image of him dropping to his knees kept playing across her mind. He had been shot with the silver bullet. He had told her not to long before that about silver being lethal to his kind. Tears sprang to her eyes at the thought that Charles could possibly be lying dead in the same spot she had left him. The tears came harder, flowing down her cheeks and dropping to the dirty concrete floor. She let out a loud sob.

"Oh Charles, you can't be dead." Elsa sniffed; she had not even told him that she loved him. She had fallen in love with him in only a matter of days. She was terrified of letting him know, in fear that he wouldn't feel the same way; or she would scare him away. She gave herself a mental kick; she should have had the courage to tell him. Life was too short. Now it seemed that she would never get the chance to let him know how she felt about him. Elsa could no longer keep her grief in check, she began to weep uncontrollably. Sadness, regret, loss and just about every other bad emotion she could possibly feel washed over her. Through her tears, she looked around the room again. Where was she anyway? She wondered if she was even still on Great Harbor Cay. Just when fresh tears started to flow, the door burst open causing her to jump. Her eyes flew to the door.

The crazy man who had kidnapped her stepped in. She glowered at him. If looks could kill, he would have dropped dead before her. "I see you are finally awake my dear."

"Where am I? And don't you *my dear* me," she spat.

He chuckled, "Well aren't you feisty. You don't need to worry about where you are right now little girl."

Elsa pulled at the iron cuffs around her hand. "You had better let me go or-or-"

"Or what? Your boyfriend is going to eat me?" He chuckled, sending her a mocking look, "I'm sorry to tell you this but your demon boyfriend is dead."

"Don't call him that! He's no demon. You killed a good man." You deserve to rot in hell for it," Elsa hissed.

The man seethed, taking angry steps toward her. He pointed his finger in her face, "If that is so, you should be right down there with me, for carrying on with that *abomination*."

Elsa glared at him. She was not a violent person by nature; but if she was not chained to the floor, she would have attacked him. "What abomination are you talking about?"

"Your boyfriend was a shape shifter, not a human being; an atrocity of nature."

"You are seriously psychotic."

"You know very well what he was."

Elsa shook her head and lifted her chin in defiance. She would deny that Charles was anything but human, to the death. There was no way this man was going to get her to admit anything. "I have no idea what you are talking about. Have you ever considered getting professional help from a psychiatrist? It sounds to me like you are mentally ill."

The man growled and stepped toward her; he delivered a slap to her face with the back of his hand. The blow sent Elsa to the floor. Pain spread across the right side of her face; she blinked rapidly, more tears springing to her eyes. He loomed over her and sneered, "I am not crazy. I know there are disgusting creatures out there. I have proof. I have been suspicious of your boyfriend since I first saw him on the ship; but I wasn't sure what he was. The night we docked on this island, I spotted him sneaking into the woods. Who sneaks around the woods at night, if they are up to anything good? Anyway I followed him and I saw two giant wolves."

Elsa glared at him with disdain, "So, what proof do you have? Did you see him transform into a wolf."

The man paused, "Well no, but I knew it was him. He was one of the wolves that I saw I know it."

Elsa rolled her eyes, "Yeah that would hold up in the court of law," she spat. "You sir are full of crap."

"Shut up! I know they exist!" He shouted, conviction evident in his tone. There was no convincing him otherwise.

Elsa decided to plead with him, "Pease just let me go. You have already killed Charles." Her voice hitched when she thought of Charles being dead. "What do you want me for?"

He turned to her,"I was told to take you alive."

Elsa's head shot up, "What? By who?"

He glowered, "Quiet! You ask too many questions."

"Are you working with someone? Who? I'm sure he or she has a name. Since I'm not going anywhere, you might as well tell me. " Elsa looked at him expectantly, hoping that he would share some information.

"All you need to know is that there is another person on the ship who shares my beliefs. All abominations of nature must die. They are corrupting our human genes. Taking our women for themselves, procreating and bring more monsters into the world." He paused and looked at her, "I suppose it is not too late for you. Although you have been soiled by that shape shifter, you can still be redeemed. There is hope for you yet."

Elsa rolled her eyes; she had to find a way to get away from this insane person. "What's your name?"

"I am Gordon Reeves, defender of the human race and soldier of Christ."

Oh boy, he is far gone, Elsa thought. "Mr. Reeves, since you think there is some kind of redemption for me; why not let me go?"

"Because my dear, my partner gave me specific instructions to keep you here."

"Your partner or your *boss*?"

"I am my own boss!"

"You poor fool," Elsa muttered.

Gordon whipped his head around, "What was that?"

Elsa shook her head, "Nothing Mr. Reeves, you carry on." Elsa's heart dropped. She wasn't going to get away from the insane Gordon Reeves. She wondered who the other person was. What could he or she possibly want with her? She had no enemies; she had lived a simple lonely life prior to this vacation. What she would give to be back in Georgia, in her crappy apartment and her boring job. She wished she had never come on this vacation. But, she would never have met Charles if she hadn't. In all her pain and fear, Elsa smiled and her heart warmed. The few days she had with Charles had been worth all her fear and misery now. If she could go back in time, she would not do anything differently.

She sat quietly on the floor, in the dark cold room; waiting for whatever would come next. She no longer cared what happened to her. If Charles was dead, she might as well be too. She used her memories of Charles to comfort and warm her, until she got away from here- one way or the other.

Charles finally made it to the hotel. He stumbled into his room and collapsed on the bed. All he needed was sleep and he would be as good as new by morning. He fell asleep as soon as his head hit the pillow. He had one thought before he slipped into slumber. *Elsa.*

Charles's eyes snapped open. Faint light filtered in through the curtains. He bolted upright in bed and looked around. He was in the hotel room. His gaze shifted to the window; it was early morning. It was time for him to get up and start his search for Elsa. He wondered if Victor had been able to locate where she had been taken. He jumped out of bed and lifted his shirt. His bullet wound was already healed. There was no evidence that he was ever injured.

Charles walked to the window to peer outside. The place was already buzzing with activity. People were having breakfast while some laundered on the beach. They were all making the best out of their situation; they were grounded on this island. Their cruise ship had been docked at Great Harbor Cay indefinitely, until the investigation of the mysterious deaths on board was completed. But things had escalated since they were grounded on the island because the killings did not stop. First a native girl was killed; and then the ship's captain. Charles sighed; there was no telling who would be next.

He knew very well who was behind the murders, but he just couldn't seem to get his hands on the man. He was very smart and cunning. Every time there was a confrontation, the man managed to slip away. It would be a bit easier if he knew what the man looked like. He always wore a mask when he was in human form; and he knew how to conceal his scent. Neither Charles nor Victor could pin the man down. He growled in frustration and moved from the window. It was time to go back into the woods to meet with Victor. He had to be there waiting by now.

Charles stepped out into the humid tropical air. Just when he turned to walk in the direction of the woods he heard his name. "Charles dear, over here!" *Damn it.* He did not need the delay right now. He turned around to see Tabitha and Arnold waving excitedly. He strolled over to the older couple who Elsa had made friends with; and plastered a bright smile on to his face.

"Good morning Tabitha, Arnold. How are you?"

"We're great, but we have been worried about Elsa," Tabitha said. "How is she? Is she feeling any better?"

Charles remembered that Elsa had told them she wasn't feeling well yesterday. But he knew that was just her ploy to get away because she was upset with him. "Uh, she is doing much better today. But she is still in bed."

Tabitha placed her hand on her jaw, "Oh the poor dear, we should pay her a visit," she turned to her husband, "Right Arnie?"

Arnold nodded in agreement, "If she can manage visitors."

Alarmed, Charles replied, "I think it's best if she rests. I know she will come down and have dinner with you two if she is feeling up to it later. Let her sleep."

Tabitha sighed, "Yes, I suppose you're right, we should leave her alone for now." She smiled brightly, "Ok well, give her our greeting and let her know we miss her."

Charles smiled, "I will most certainly do that Tabitha." He turned and walked off, relieved that he had thwarted the couples plan to visit Elsa. He glanced around briefly to see if anyone was watching; and sauntered off into the thickly foliaged woods. He walked quietly and cautiously. The man who had shot him was still running around out here, there was no telling if he would just appear out of nowhere like he did last night. He also didn't know if the mysterious shifter would show himself. He sniffed the air, smelling for any sign that he was not alone. The only scent he picked up was Victor's. The man must be waiting for him in the distance.

Victor turned as Charles padded forward, his eye roamed over the younger man. "You look well patched up."

"Thanks again for saving my life."

Victor nodded and shrugged, "I want Elsa so be happy, and you seem to make her happy. So, saving your life doesn't necessarily mean I like you," he teased.

Charles grinned, "I never begged you like me. I don't like you much either, old man"

The older man laughed. "I found her. She is being held in an old building on the other end of the island."

Charles breathed a sigh of relief. He was happy to hear that Elsa was still alive. Hope bloomed inside him; he would have her back in his arms in just a short while. "What are we still standing her for? Let's go get her back. Lead the way." Charles began to remove his clothing, ready to take his wolf form.

"Wait, we shouldn't; it is safer if we avoid shifting in broad day light. There is a chance we will be seen. Two giant wolves running around a tropical island is much cause for suspicion."

"You are right." Charles didn't even stop to think about that, his urgent need to get to Elsa clouded his rational thoughts. They would get there much faster in their wolf form, but he would have to be patient, for their own protection. There was already one person who had discovered their existence; they did not need any more humans hunting them down. The rumor of non-humans among them was already planted by the crazy man who had shot him. Of someone, saw wolves in the area, suspicion would most certainly arise; then they would have more crazy fanatics to worry about.

They moved quickly forward. The island wasn't very big, so they would still get there in no time. Charles was growing more anxious by the minute. He wondered if Elsa was alright. She probably thought he was dead. There had been sheer terror in her voice when he had dropped to his knees after being shot. He pictured her being terrorized by that mad man; and let out a low growl. His would ripples beneath his skin. There would be hell to pay, for taking Elsa away from him.

Charles followed Victor until he stopped a good distance away from an abandoned brick building. The structure looked like it was on the verge of collapsing. "We can't just rush in, we need to find out if there is anyone else in there," Victor suggested.

Charles nodded; they had to tread lightly in case there was more than one fanatic wielding guns loaded with silver bullets. "Let's watch the building from here for a little while." They crouched behind the bushed and watched the old decrepit building. Charles came at attention when he saw someone exit the building. It was the man who had shot him. Charles had to keep his wolf in check; the animal inside of him was ready to attack. They watched as the man paced back and forth, muttering to himself. Occasionally he glanced at his watch and looked in their direction. "He is expecting someone," Charles observed.

"So it seems. I say we wait and see who it is." They moved out of the path that anyone coming in that direction would take. Both men covered themselves with dirt and leaves, in an attempt to conceal their scent. It was possible that the other wolf shifter was roaming the island.

They waited for hours, watching and waiting. Finally, footsteps were heard approaching. A young man walked right past them and stepped into the clearing. Charles recognized the man. He was one of the ship's crew members. Charles recalled seeing him in some kind of uniform. The man holding Elsa captive came back outside. "Justin, what took you so long?" He asked the new comer angrily. "I was expecting you hours ago."

"Hey, if I were you, I would watch my tone Gordon," he warned lowly. "Now do you have the girl inside?"

"She is there. What is so important about her anyway?"

"That's none of your concern, old man," he hissed.

"It is my concern since I was the one who had to go though the trouble of getting her."

"I told you, you will be compensated for that."

"How exactly are you going to do that? The shape shifter you promised to deliver into my hands is dead, I shot him myself."

Justin stared down his nose at the man, "Don't worry yourself old man, I happen to know that there is another one on the island. I will deliver him to you."

Gordon's eyes widened, "Another on? My God, we are surrounded by monsters." Gordon threw his hand up dramatically.

Justin's head whipped around as if he detected something. He searched the area, and then turned back to Gordon. "I need you to keep her here a little longer."

"No way, I have held up my end of the bargain. It's time for you to do your own dirty work."

Justin grabbed Gordon by the neck and squeezed. "You will do as I tell you old man, or I will rip you head off." He released his grip, "Have I made myself clear?" Gordon cowered before the younger man and nodded. Justin sauntered off in the opposite direction.

"That's him," Victor said. "That is the man who has been following Elsa."

Charles turned to him, his interest peeked. "What are you talking about who is he?"

Victor turned to him and sighed, "That is the man who killed your father two years ago.

Charles's heart stopped. He had just seen his father's murder. He had been standing just within walking distance. Anger washed over him, all he had to do was catch up with the now and kill him. He took a calming breath. He had to rescue Elsa and get her to safety. Then he would worry about his father's murderer. "What the hell does he Elsa have to do with that man? What does he want with her?"

"I found out years ago that he has been making enquiries about the Greys, Elsa's parents."

Charles's brow furrowed. "We can discus all of this later. Let get Elsa out of there.

Chapter Three

Elsa sat up gingerly; every inch of her was in pain. By now the bruise on her right cheek had transformed into an unsightly shade of black and blue. She rolled her neck and shoulders experimentally. *Ouch.* She was stiff and sore from lying on the hard concrete floor for hours. Her captor couldn't have been thoughtful enough to provide a cushion? If he was going to kill her, he could have at least provided her with a little comfort. She pulled at the chains on her wrist experimentally. She dropped her hands in frustration; she had attempted to pull her hands free about a million times already. She looked around, hadn't anyone noticed her absence yet? Her heart fell, of course not. She was only one of two thousand passengers that had been grounded on the island' her absence would not have gone noticed; only Tabitha and Arnold would miss her, but it was much too soon.

Has Charles's body not been found yet? She dropped her head and burst into tears again. She had been crying on and off since last night, every time she thought about Charles no longer being in this world. It hurt even more because she blamed herself. Her tears were now flowing uncontrollably. If they had left the waterfall the minute Charles had suggested, he would still be alive. But no, she just had to stay satisfy her sexual cravings. Now the man she loved was dead and she might as well be too. What was a world without him in it?

She had led a mostly lonely life before meeting him, but now she could not bear the thought of a world without him. She sniffed loudly. Was that talking she heard? She was positive she had heard more than one voices. She cocked her ear and strained to hear. "Do you have the girl?" that was all she was able to pick up. She assumed she was the girl in question. So that was the man who Gordon had mentioned. What in the world did he want with her? She was sure she didn't know whoever it was out there.

Just then the door burst open with such force; it hit and bounced off the wall. The old building trembled with the impact. Elsa peered up at the ceiling afraid the decrepit structure would collapse on their heads. Gordon stomped inside, visibly upset. He breathed so hard his nose flared out, and his skin was flushed a bright red. He muttered to himself, something about the nerve of someone. He was obviously distressed about something. Elsa snorted; she had no sympathy for the man. "Trouble in paradise, Mr. Reeves?"

He swung around to look at her, his eyes bulging with growing anger. He walked toward her, finger outstretched, "*You*. You are the cause of this."

Elsa gasped as he drew closer, "The cause of what? I haven't done anything." How could she have been at fault for whatever he spoke of? She had been chained to the floor the entire time. "Have you for some reason forgotten that you chained me to the floor Gordon?"

"I should just kill you and be done with it. That would show Justin that I am not afraid of him."

"I-I don't know any J-Justin," Elsa stuttered growing more nervous by the second. "Maybe you have the wrong girl."

Gordon shook his head, "It is definitely you he wants." He sneered, "The man had the nerve to threaten me, after I have been the one doing all of his dirty work. I am going to kill you, and continue God's work of wiping out the monsters on my own."

Elsa gaped at him, wide eyed. It was now evident that the man had completely slipped over into insanity. He loomed over her and she drew back. She panicked when he drew a knife from his belt. She was not going to go down without a fight. She leaned back and kicked him in the gut with all of her might. Gordon grunted and staggered backward with the impact. The knife he held fell from his grip and scattered across the floor.

He lunged after her again, pure hatred and rage in his eye. Elsa let out a piercing screams as he pushed her to the floor. She moaned when her head hit the hard floor. Before she could recover from her shock, Gordon wrapped his beefy hands around her neck. She tried to fight back, thrashing and kicking. She tried to loosen his grip on her neck, but her hands were restricted by the chains. Gordon squeezed until Elsa's world started to darken. *This is it, I'm going to die*, she thought. Who would have thought that this was how she would go out? She would be killed by the hands of the man who had shot and killed her lover; on a tropical island in the Caribbean. She nearly laughed; the events of her death were very different from the dull life she had led, that was for sure.

She gasped for breath and her vision started to blur due to lack of oxygen. "I love you Charles," she whispered. She had not gotten the chance to tell him. So, she figured she would utter the words out loud before she died; release them into the atmosphere in the event that his spirit might hear them. Suddenly, Gordon was ripped away from her. Her lungs expanded with much needed oxygen, as she sucked in a deep breath. She couldn't see what was happening, but she heard Gordon let out a strangled shriek; then there was silence, She wondered if Justin had come back to kill him, and then her? She propped up on her elbow to see what was happening. Gordon lay lifeless on the concrete floor in a pool of blood. His eyes were open in a blank stared. She shuddered at the sight of him. Her gaze drifted upward to the man standing over Gordon. *Charles?* She blinked rapidly. Oh no, she was hallucinating. Her oxygen deprived brain was playing ticks on her; or she wanted to see Charles so badly that she conjured him up. Maybe she was seeing a ghost.

The object of her hallucination rushed to her side, he knelt beside her and grabbed her shoulders. "Elsa are you alright?" She only stared up at him, still dazed. He shook her slightly, "Talk to me Elsa."

"Are you real?" she asked weakly.

She felt the chains on her wrist being pulled; the cuffs around her wrist fell open. Charles ran his fingers gently over her discoloured wrists. "Yes, I'm real," he breathed.

Elsa hurled herself into his arms and immediately burst into tears. He caught her and bought her to her feet. She sobbed into his neck, "Oh Charles, I thought you were dead." Her body was wracked with the intensity of her sobs.

He smoothed her hair. "I'm here Elsa, I'm here." He whispered. He was relieved to have her back in his arms.

"We should get out of here you two," Victor said from the doorway.

Elsa's gaze flew to the door. She gasped and hid herself behind Charles. Oh my God, Charles its Mr. Creepy. What is he doing here?"

Victor gave her a confused look, "Mr. *what?*"

"What do you want from us?" she asked, peeking out from behind Charles.

He threw both hands up, "I'm here to help Elsa."

"How do you know my name?" She looked up at Charles and whispered, "He really has been stalking me; he knows my name and everything."

Charles reassured her, "It's ok Elsa, he really is on our side. He is the one who found where you were taken, and led me to you. He is right; we need to get out of here now."

They moved through the woods, back to the hotel. The day had transformed to dark night. They walked for what seemed like forever. Elsa threw Victor suspicious glanced the entire journey back. The man could not help but feel a bit uncomfortable, so he maintained a safe distance. Her heated stared only lessened when Charles let her know that Victor had saved his life when he had been shot. She then looked upon him with grudging gratitude. *It still doesn't mean I have to like him.*

Elsa sagged against Charles, as the hotel came in to view. She was immensely relieved they were almost at their destination. Exhaustion swept over her; all she wanted to do was collapse on the bed and sleep until they could leave the island. She was ready to leave the island paradise which had had turned to hell. She doubted she would ever set foot on a ship again, for as long as she lived.

Charles turned to Victor, "Just give us some time, then you can stop by our room."

Victor nodded, "I will be there soon then."

Elsa blanched. Had Charles just invited her stalker to their room? She watched as Victor disappeared into the darkness. She looked up at Charles, "Are you insane? Why would you invite him to our room?"

Charles sighed, "I told he is on our side. He has something to explain to you. Just trust me, will you?"

Elsa opened her mouth to reply, but snapped it shut. What could Victor possibly have to say to her? Was he going to apologize for stalking her on the ship? She sighed; she supposed if Charles trusted him, Victor couldn't be too bad. She was grateful that he had saved Charles's life.

As soon as Charles pushed the room door open, he swept her into his arms and carried her to the bathroom. "Let's get you cleaned up." He placed her on her feet and began to undress slowly undress her. He then, proceeded to remove his clothes. "Come," he took her hand and assisted her into the bathtub. Elsa closed her eyes and revelled in the feeling of his strong hands washing her hair and bathing her. Elsa smiled; she had never received such treatment from a man before. She could get use to it.

She turned to wrap her arms around his neck. Lifting herself she found his lips with her own. Charles moved his lips over her gently. "Make love to me Charles," she whispered. He immediately lifted her on to him. Elsa wound her legs around his waist, and planted soft kisses against his jaw and neck as he strode to the bedroom. Their wet bodies tumbled onto the bed, rolling so that Elsa straddled him. She wasted no time; she lifted herself over his hard shaft and slid down slowly, inch by inch. Charles gritted his teeth, fighting to remain still as Elsa's tight sheath slowly engulfed his length. The sweet feeling was too much and he lost control. He pushed his hips upward, burying himself inside her softness. Elsa gasped at the feeling of the sudden fullness.

Charles palmed her breasts bringing his head up to take one nipple into his mouth. Shockwaves coursed through Elsa at the contact of his tongue on the beaded flesh. Charles was overwhelmed with passion; he laid his head back on the bed and ran his palms over her soft skin, worshiping every inch of her body. He stared in amazement of the erotic picture she made above him. Her head was thrown back, her lips slightly parted, pleasure written on her features; her small breasts bounced slightly with every slow up and down movement of her hips. She looked like a sensual goddess riding him to the brink of ecstasy. "Elsa, you are so beautiful," he breathed.

He rolled her on to her back in one swift motion. He lifted her hands above her head, and plunged into her with faster strokes. She closed her eyes as pleasure washed over her.

"Look at me Elsa."

Her eyes flew open and he held her gaze. Elsa arched her hips and moaned, as the tension that had built up in her core was released and pleasure wracked her body. She let out a shriek as her orgasm rippled through her. Charles pushed into her one more time and slipped over the edge. His body shuddered as he collapse on top of her. Their breaths sounded harsh in the silence of the room. He moved to roll himself off of her, but she stopped him, holding on to him tightly. "I'm too heavy," he whispered.

"No, you feel perfect." They lay intertwined in each other's embrace for a few minutes. They were reluctant to let go, after coming so close to losing one another.

"We should get dressed, Victor will be here any minute," Charles uttered, breaking the silence.

Elsa blew out a breath, "Oh right, *him.*" She was not pleased. Nevertheless she got up and got dressed. A few moments later a knock sounded on the door. Elsa scoffed, "Great he's here."

Charles leaned down to plant a kiss on her forehead. "Please try to be nice." He strolled to the door and let Victor in.

Victor nodded to Charles and turned to Elsa. "Hello again Elsa."

"Hello Victor," she responded coldly. "Come in, have a seat." *Right where I can see you.* She was tempted to perform a body search like a security guard. *If he makes even the slightest wrong move I'll* ... Elsa rolled her eyes and plopped on the edge of the bed; she had no idea what she would do.

Victor held a seat on a sofa. He couldn't help but feel uncomfortable with the daggers Elsa threw at him with each glance. He blew out a breath; it was going to be a long night.

Elsa narrowed her gaze at the older man, "So Charles told me you have something to explain to me." She couldn't wait to hear what he came out with.

"Uh yes; there are several things actually." Victor took a deep breath. He had no idea where to even start.

"Ok, please start with why you were stalking me on the ship."

Victor shook his head, "I wasn't stalking you, I was watching over you."

Elsa cocked an eyebrow and snorted, "That you were, and very creepily too."

Victor sighed, "Let me start from the beginning. "I'm your god father. Your father was my best friend. Sadness was suddenly cast over his features

Elsa gawked at him, her mouth hanging open. "I beg your pardon." Did he just say he was her god father?

"The day he died, I held him in my arms until he took his last breath. He asked me to look after you and I promised him that I would."

Elsa swallowed, "Lies. Why should I believe anything you say?"

Victor captured her gaze. "Because it is the truth," he said softly.

Elsa shook her head; she suddenly found it hard to catch her breath. Her parents were a very sensitive topic. "What you claim makes no sense. How could you have held any conversation with my father? Both and my mother died in a car crash," she swallowed, "They died instantly." Charles walked over to sit beside her; he took her hand into his and squeezed.

Victor continued, "That's what you were told. Do you remember the weekend you spent at your childhood friend's house?" She nodded. How could she forget the weekend she lost her parents? "Your parents travelled to England."

Elsa was confused, "I don't understand. Why?"

Victor glanced at Charles who nodded, "Tell her. She deserves to know the truth. She handled the revelation of me being a shape shifter, she can handle this."

Elsa looked at the two men, "Tell me what?" She looked at Victor and narrowed her eyes, "Spit it out."

"Your father was a wolf shifter. He was called by the council of the pack that he was a part of before he married your mother." Elsa merely stared at Victor, completely dumfounded. She couldn't seem to find her tongue. "It is against the rules for a shifter to take a human mate. Many of us disregard that rule without consequence. But, our pack was polluted with old fashioned shifters, they were extremely fanatical. They believed in maintain the purity of our species. When the demanded that your father travel to England to stand before them, I told him not to. But he was tired of running; he wanted his family to live in peace." Victor stopped to take a breath, he found it difficult not to get emotional talking about what happen to the man he loved as a brother.

"Please, continue," Elsa encouraged softly.

"Your mother insisted on going with him. She was just as determined as her husband to settle things once and for all. I received word of the council's intentions; but before I could get to your father to warn him, your mother was already dead and your father was barely hanging on to life." Victor looked down at his hands, remembering how his friend's blood had covered his palms. He made me promise to keep you safe. I have been watching over you since you were nine years old Elsa. I even followed you when you left Pennsylvania to attend school in Georgia. I have watched you grow into a beautiful, strong woman. Your parents would be proud."

Tears formed in Elsa's eyes again. "But how have you been following me? I have never seen you before the first day of the cruise."

"I have been fulfilling my promise to your father from the background."

Elsa sniffed, "If you loved my father so much, why didn't you take me?"

Victor let out a breath, "God knows I wanted to Elsa. But I couldn't bring you into my world, it was too dangerous. I asked your uncle Henry to take you, he refused. He said you were a reminder of why his brother died. But I managed to convince him."

"Uncle Henry was a shifter?"

"He was," Victor nodded. "He never approved of the union between your parents. He was also stuck in the pack's old ways. You being human with the shifter gene was unacceptable to him. "

Elsa was in a state of shock. That explained her uncle's cold disdain towards her. "Ok, I'm stuck on the part where I'm half wolf. Can shift and do all the cool stuff you guys do?"

Victor chuckled, "I'm afraid not. You only have the gene. But that means it is possible for you to be converted; it has been done successfully in the past. It is tedious process which involves draining your blood and-

"Whoa there, ok enough of that," Elsa interrupted. I really don't need to know about that right now." Elsa was horrified, this conversion process sounded painful. "Um Victor, I know you made a promise to my father and all, but did you really have to follow me on my vacation?"

A serious expression crossed his face, "I received word some years ago that your existence was stumbled up on and there are still a few members remaining of my pack who seek to rid the world of those they consider impure. Someone was sent to kill you Elsa and he is still trying. I trailed the shifter that was sent to kill you right on to a damn cruise ship."

"Speaking of the ship; why did you attack me Victor?"Elsa asked, confused.

"I didn't. I was hiding in the shadows, watching over you as usual and I knew the other shifter was headed straight to you, so I grabbed you to get you out of his direct path."

"What about when you came after Charles and me *again* that night in the corridor?"

"I was actually going after Charles. I knew he was a wolf shifter and I though he seduced you to harm you in some way. It turns out I was wrong; he has actually been protecting you better than I have. "

Elsa blushed, "Oh." She was embarrassed that the man she just found out was her god father knew about her sexual relationship with Charles.

"Plus he was hunting me down to kill me, so I also thought he found out about your connection to me," Victor added.

Elsa gasped and whipped around to confront Charles. "You've been *hunting* my god father?"

"I thought he killed my father," Charles defended himself. He threw Victor a look promising retaliation.

Victor rushed to provide clarity, "Which I didn't of course. It was actually Justin, the same man who is after you Elsa. Charles's and your father were also friends. Justin thought his father knew where you were." He directed his attention to Charles, "The night you found me standing over your father, I was trying to find out why Justin had attacked him."

Charles nodded, "He said something about the girl before he die. I had no idea what he was talking about at the time. But I do now," he said look at Elsa.

Elsa got up abruptly and walked to stare out the window. "So I'm responsible for the death of Charles's father." She felt terrible. "I'm also the reason why innocent people have been dying on the ship *and* this island."

Charles appeared behind her and turned her around, forcing her to look at him. "Don't you dare blame yourself for any of this. You're hands are clean. Do you hear me?"

He gazed shifted away from his, "But your father was killed because Justin wanted to get to me. How can you even look at me Charles?" she asked, tears filling her eyes.

"For the last time, it's not your fault. Don't do this to yourself." He lowered his head to capture her lips. Victor coughed loudly from across the room. Elsa and Charles turned to look at him, shocked; as if they had forgotten he was there. Charles's hands dropped to his sides as he glowered at Victor, who returned his heated stare.

Elsa looked from Charles to Victor. She shook her head, "This entire thing is so insane." There were so many twists and turns to the story Victor had just told her. She was half wolf for crying out loud. She gave a mental snort, no wonder she was terrible people skills. She glanced at Charles; they were connected in more ways than she thought; their fathers had been friends. Even though Charles had reassured her, she still felt guilty. So many people had died because of Justin's search for her. How many more innocent people would die? This had to end. Her gaze drifted to Victor who sat staring into space. He seemed so sad. Her heart softened, "Um, Victor?" His haze swung to her. "I'm sorry for treating you so terribly, and I apologize for the nickname as well."

"Huh? What nickname?" He glared at Charles who smothered a laugh. Then he remembered what she had called him after they found her in the abandoned building. "Wait let me guess, is it Mr. Creepy."

Elsa flushed, "Well, you have to admit you following me around is undeniably creepy. But I really am sorry. You are a pretty decent guy and I appreciate you watching over me all these year. You're like my very own fairy god father."

Victor chuckled, "You are your mother's daughter. You inherited her sense of humor." Elsa beamed, pleased with the knowledge.

Chapter Four

"We have to stop Justin, once and for all," Elsa said, moving to stand in the middle of the room. "The blood spill has gone too far."

"I agree," Victor nodded.

Charles rubbed his hand along his jaw, "The man is fast and cunning. We need to play it smart."

"I have a plan." Both men turned to give Elsa their full attention. "I'm the one he really wants, right? So let him have me. I can act as the bait, so that you two can take him down. "

Both men chorused, "Absolutely not."

Charles turned to her, "Have you lost your bloody mind?" His accent was more pronounced with his anger. "There is no way I will allow you to go anywhere near Justin."

"For once I agree with your boyfriend, Elsa" Victor added.

She rolled her eyes. She though using herself as bait was a brilliant idea. "I don't hear either of you throwing out any ideas. If I can get him alone, you two can easily get him.

Victor considered for a moment, "I think you are on to something Elsa."

Charles swung to the older man, outraged. "I see you have joined your god daughter in the land of the insane. There is one major problem. The man is a wolf shifter he will sniff us out from a mile away."

Elsa nibbled on her fingernails, deep in thought. "Does water mask your scent?"

Victor nodded, "Enough of it can, yes."

Elsa smiled broadly, "I know how this can work. The waterfall; I can lead Justin out to the woods and straight to the waterfall, where you two will be submerged in the pond, waiting for the right moment to pounce."

Victor gave a clap, "That is brilliant Elsa. It just might work," he beamed at her proudly.

Charles shook his head, still not comfortable with the idea. "You two are out of your minds. How do we know Justin won't kill you on sight Elsa?"

She shook her head, "He won't. Gordon told me that he wanted me alive. He might very well try to kill me, but not right away. He either has something he wants to say or do first. Which gives you guys the window to step in and take him down before he makes his attempt."

Charles sighed heavily, "It's still too dangerous."

Elsa held on to his hand, "Come on Charles, this can work. With you there, I will be safe. I know you won't let him hurt me. We have to put an end to this. If we can somehow keep him alive and hand him over to the police, their investigation will come to an end, and we can finally get off of this island."

Victor stood up, "I would feel better removing the man from the world completely, but handing him to the authorities can work too. I for one would love to get the hell of this island. We also have an advantage; we now know what he looks like in human form, but he doesn't know that we do. It can work."

Elsa smiled, satisfied. "Then it's settled, we put our plan into action tomorrow night then."

Charles opened his mouth to refute once again, but what he saw in Elsa's eyes stopped him. He held her gaze; there he saw determination and defiance. There was no convincing her not to go ahead with her plan. He sighed, he had no choice but to go along with it.

Charles stood leaning against the window. He peered out into the darkness. He still brooded over the plan that Victor and Elsa were so eager to carry out. How could he just stand by and watch while the woman he loved walk right into the hands of the man who wants her dead? He ran a hand over his face, he hated the damn plan. He had come so close to losing her too many times already. So, he was a bag of nerves thinking about her He shook his head, the only thing he could now was ensure that she did not get hurt. He would protect her with his life.

He felt Elsa's arms wind around him. She pressed her body against his back. "I know what you're thinking about Charles. You need to stop worrying. Come to bed, you need to rest." She paused, "Or we can engage in other activities if you are not ready to go to sleep yet." Charles inhaled sharply; he was instantly aroused by her suggestive words.

He turned around, to look down at her and grinned. "I'm not quite ready to sleep yet. I believe I owe you something."

She tipped her head sideway, her brows furrowing in confusion, "What's that?"

He swept her up off the floor, causing her to shriek in surprise. "I can show you better that I can tell you." He took long strides across the room and threw her unceremoniously onto the bed. She giggled when she bounced up and down. Charles knelt on the floor and took hold of her feet, pulling her to the edge of the bed. He hooked his fingers in the waist band of her skirt and pulled it off; her underwear went next. She still had no idea what he was up to.

He pushed her thighs apart and began to kiss his way up her thighs, moving dangerously close to her most secret place. Elsa propped up on her elbows as it dawned on her exactly what he was about to do. Her eyes widened. *Oh.* Charles planted a kiss on her sensitive bud. Her legs clamped shut, in surprise. "Charles I've never... no one has ever..."

He opened her legs again, "I know baby, relax." She lay down, her breath quickening. His tongue darted out to stroke her clitoris. Elsa cried out. He skilfully pleasured her with his tongue, bringing her to the brink of ecstasy. She moaned, "Oh wow, Charles." With one more stroke of his tongue, Elsa exploded. Her orgasm tore through her, lifting her body up off of the bed. Before she could come down from her high, Charles stood up and swiftly discarded his clothes. He flipped her over flipped her over and bought her to her knees. He grabbed her hips and plunged into her hot sheath. *"Charles,"* Elsa whimpered when he filled her. He moved with slow, deep strokes. Her muscles gripped him tightly and he threw his head back. The intensity of his pleasure caused his wolf to ripple beneath the surface; he lost control. His teeth lengthened to razor sharp fangs and his eyes transformed. He let out a feral growl and bent down to clamp his teeth over Elsa's shoulder, pinning her in place.

She gasped and stiffened; panic rose up inside of her chest. Was he going to bit her? She instantly relaxed when he reached a hand up to caress her face then her back, his hips still moving slowly. What had she been thinking? Charles would never hurt her. The alpha in him had taken over and he was merely excising his dominance as wolves usually did when mating. The pace of his hips increased and plunged into her over and over. Elsa soon felt another ripple moving through her, "Charles I'm going to- *oh my*." Her entire body trembled as pleasure overwhelmed her. Charles slammed into her again, and shouted out as he found his release.

He pulled away from her and fell onto the bed. Elsa collapsed beside him and he pulled her into his arms. "I'm sorry if I scared you," he said into the silence.

She peeked up at him through her lashes. "You mean when you went all wolf man on me?"

He covered his eyes with a hand. "*Wolf man?*" he groaned.

She giggled, "It's ok. I was only scared for a second. I actually liked it."

"You are the most amazing woman I have ever met Elsa." He stared at her in wonder. She had accepted everything about him. She had the biggest heart. He kissed her forehead. He wanted to keep her with him forever. But he knew his time with her was approaching its end. A cold feeling settled in the pit of his stomach at the thought. They would soon be able to leave this island. When they reached Miami she would go back to Georgia. As much as he need and loved her, he couldn't ask her to give up her life in Georgia to be with him. She had her own home and a job and friends. It was selfish of him to even think about ask her to stay with him.

He sighed. How the hell was he going to let her go when the time came? *You can't.* His wolf spoke to him; they both needed her. It dawned on him that had not even told her how he felt. Maybe if he expressed that he was in love with her, she would choose to stay with him. The time was now; he was ready to tell her how he felt. "Elsa?" He received no answer. He looked down to find her fast asleep. Of course she had fallen asleep; she must be exhausted after what she had been through. He studied the woman in his arms. Her long eyelashes fanned her cheeks and her full lips were curved in a half smile. Her red tresses spread out across his chest and spilled onto the sheet. She looked so young and innocent. *She is young and innocent.* She was a mere twenty-three years old; she had her entire life ahead of her. He had to make sure that she got the chance to life her life. He had to get rid of the threat to her.

Charles was awakened by Elsa thrashing and moaning beside him. He propped up to study her; she was fast asleep. She was in the throes of a nightmare. She swung her head from side to side "Charles don't go," she moaned softly. He wrapped his arms around her and drew her into his embrace. She instantly stopped flaying about and snuggled closer to him. He leaned down to whisper in her ear, "I'm not going anywhere, Elsa. I love you."

Elsa moaned as she gingerly sat up in bed. She had been awakened by her intestines protesting loudly. She was reminded that she had not eaten anything in quite a while. She let out another moan when she tried to move. Her entire body was sore, reminding her of the concrete floor she has spent hours lying down on. The right side of her face stung, she could see the swelling of her skin when she looked down. She knew there was a large hideous bruise there. Gordon had really done a number on her. Her throat ached when she swallow, she knew that there was large bruise around her neck from nearly being strangled to death. She looked down at her wrists which sported black and blue colored marks. She was one big walking bruise.

She turned to glanced down at Charles. He was still asleep. She smiled slightly; he looked younger than his thirty year when he was relaxed. He was always so on edge worrying about her safety. He didn't have to stress about protecting her, but he did and she loved him so much for caring. She wondered if he felt the same way as she felt about him. She wanted to hear him tell her that he loved her so badly. She had even dreamt that he said the words last night. She sighed when she thought about returning home. She and Charles wolf be no more. She would go back to her dull, lonely life and he would continue with his billionaire lifestyle. He probably wouldn't even remember her after a while, she thought sadly. But she would never forget Charles. She would always love him, even if they were worlds apart. She would have memories of him to keep her warm at nights.

Her stomach growled again, "Ok ok, I'll eat something soon."

"Who are you talking to?"

Elsa shrieked, she nearly jumped out of her skin. Her head whipped around, causing her to wince. He sat up abruptly, concern on his face, "What's wrong? Are you in pain?"

She nodded, "Yes, my entire body hurts."

He ran his fingers gently over her bruises. Anger surged through him. If he would kill Gordon Reeves again, he would. "I'm sorry baby; the pain will go away in time."

"I thought you were asleep," she said. "You just scared the daylights out of me."

"I'm sorry. I've been up for a few minutes." He had been lying with his hands entwined behind his head, studying her intently. He had remained silent not wanting to interrupt her. She had been so deep in thought. He wondered what she had been thinking so hard about. "What were you thinking about?"

"Oh, nothing important. My stomach has been protesting since I woke up, I need food now."

He smiled, "In that case, let's go."

"My God, Elsa! What happened to you?" Tabitha stared at her in horror.

Elsa groaned as Tabitha and Arnold approached them. She had been trying to avoid the older couple this morning. Everyone else had given her strange looks; probably wondering how she had gotten all of her colourful bruises. She knew that Tabitha would make a fuss. She and Charles had deliberately come out earlier than usual, so as not to run into Tabitha and Arnold.

Arnold peered over his wife's shoulders, "Yes, what happened little girl?" He stepped around Tabitha to take a better look at Elsa. "Who did this to you?" Before Elsa could answer, his eyes swung to Charles. "You have some explaining to do, Mr. Grimm." Tabitha also turned to glower at him.

Charles looked down at the older man, amusement in his gaze. "I don't believe I have anything to explain sir."

Arnold balled his fist and shook in the air. Elsa watched I horror as he stepped toward Charles. She couldn't believe they thought Charles would lay a hand on her. She quickly stepped in front of Arnold. "Arnold wait, calm down. Charles had nothing to do with this."

"Explain how on earth you came by such damage dear," Tabitha said, her eyes roaming over Elsa's face and neck.

"Uh, I was attacked." She couldn't very well tell them that she was kidnapped by a religious fanatic with orders to do so from a wolf shifter, who wanted her dead. But, she could tell them something close to the truth.

Tabitha gasped, clutching at her chest. "By who?"

"Um, well... I decided that I wanted to explore the island yesterday evening, against Charles's advice. I was so anxious to see the beauty of the place that I ventured out on my own. I wondered into the lonely woods and a man jumped out of nowhere and attacked me." She glanced at Charles for a little assistance.

He was looking at her in amusement, a smile threatening to break through. "Go ahead Elsa, tell them what happened next."

She glared at him and turned back to Tabitha and Arnold, who were gawking at her; hanging on her every word. "Uh, so this man kept hitting me. Then he wrapped his hands around my neck and tried to strangle me. I couldn't see his face because he wore a black mask." She paused, searching for her next word. "It was a good thing that Charles noticed that I was missing and he came looking for me. He found me just in time and rescued me from my attacker. The man ran off further into the woods."

Tabitha's hands flew to her mouth. She then reached out and pulled Elsa into an oxygen restricting hug. "Oh my goodness you poor dear, you could have been killed. It's a good thing you have a strong man to protect you."

Arnold cleared his throat loudly and turned to Charles. "It seems I owe you an apology for my outburst young man. I'm lost my temper for a while there. You see, we feel protective of little Elsa."

Charles smiled, "It's quite alright Arnold, thank you for caring so much about little Elsa."

Arnold nodded, "You did good Charles."

Tabitha drew in a breath, "It seems you were the killer's next intended victim. If Charles had not save you, your body would have been discover this morning; instead of that poor man."

"What man?" Elsa asked.

"A body was found on in an abandoned building on the other side of the island. Another passenger on the ship is gone. When Charles scared the killer off, it seems he found another victim. God only knows what that mad was doing all the way out there by himself."

Charles and Elsa gave each other knowing looks. Gordon Reeves's body had been found. Charles had killed the man, because he was trying to kill her. She shuddered when she thought of how swiftly and effortlessly he had killed Gordon. It dawned on her in that moment that Charles was very deadly. Gordon lying in a pool of blood flashed across her mind. She blinked rapidly to get the image out of her head. She swallowed hard, her eyes flying to Charles. He caught her gaze and frowned. He was probably wondering why she was looking at him like that. She quickly averted her gaze. "Who knows, he should have stayed close to the hotel."

Tabitha gave a distressed look, "I can't wait for the authorities to find the murderer. Five lives have been taken by now; two on the ship and three more since we have docked her. People are really starting to panic, wondering who the killer will target next."

Elsa patted Tabitha's hand, "Don't you worry Tabitha; everything will be ok soon." She knew that because they were going to catch the scoundrel, Justin tonight. She was determined. She refused to allow him to take another life. "I'm still feeling a bit on edge after what happened yesterday. I want to just go back to our room and lie down."

"Of course dear, you go on right ahead. Arnie and I are going to retire early as well. It is simply not safe to be anymore."

"Yes that's a good Tabitha, you two should stay in your room as much as possible."

"Ok you take care dear and stay safe."

"Thanks Tabitha, you too." Elsa and Charles walked off. She elbowed Charles in the side, "Thanks for your help back there," she hissed sarcastically.

"What? You seemed to have everything under control. I think your story was great," he snickered.

"I should have let Arnold sock you in the jaw."

Charles bellowed out a laugh at the thought of Arnold attacking him. Elsa couldn't hold in her amusement any longer; she joined him, giggling uncontrollably. The thought of Arnold fighting Charles was comical. "Can you imagine?" she asked.

Charles shook his head, "I don't even want to." He continued to grin broadly. He stole a side glance at Elsa as they walked. She bought so much joy to his life. He had never laughed so much in his entire life as he had in the few days he had known Elsa. He very much wanted to keep her in his life.

Chapter Five

Elsa took a deep steadying breath. The sun had long set and the time had gotten dark. She slowly walked down the front steps of the hotel. She whimpered softly and looked back at the building. She was losing her nerves. She wanted to turn around, run back into the safety of the building and lock herself in her room until the sun came back up. She had been so pumped and ready to for what was to come tonight. She had been fuelled by anger and frustration; thinking of all the innocent lives Justin had claimed and she wanted him out of the way. But now as she walked by herself into the night, all she felt was apprehension. She headed in the direction of the woods.

Charles and Victor had long left. They should be hiding in the woods as planned. Elsa hears a twig snapped and she jumped, trying her hardest not to turn and flee, back to the hotel. "I can do this," she whispered. Footsteps sounded again, drawing closer. *Oh my God, I am freaking out right now.* She took another deep breath and held her head straight; she would not give herself away. She knew Justin was stalking her, he must have been anticipating the moment when he would find her alone, out of Charles constant company. Elsa would give anything to have Charles at her side right now. She entered the woods with her head down.

"It's not safe to be out alone," a voice said softly.

Elsa stiffened, her pulse rate going into over drive; but she remained in character. She sniffed and turned toward the voice with tears glistening in her eyes, "I know, but I was just so upset. I couldn't stay inside." She sniffed again for effect.

Justin stepped out of the shadows, "What has you so upset?" He asked concern written on his face, as he stared at her with warm friendly eyes.

Oh he is good, Elsa thought. If she had not known that he was a vicious killer she would have trusted the man. He presented himself as kind and harmless. *You're not the only one who can act you bastard.* She wiped at her eyes, "You're very kind sir but I don't want to bother you with my problems."

He smiled encouraging, "It's ok, you can tell me."

Elsa's gaze drifted to Justin's, "My boyfriend and I had a fight. I don't think we're going to get back together."

Something gleamed in Justin's eyes, but he quickly concealed it. He frowned, "I'm sorry to hear that," he said, feigning sincerity. "What are you doing so far in the woods?"

"I was heading to the waterfall. He bought me there a few days ago as a surprise. I just felt like I needed to go there tonight, as a way to find a little comfort." She started to sob, secretly pleased and proud of her new found ability for impromptu tears. "This so embarrassing, I have to go." She turned and rushed off, heading in the direction of the waterfall.

"Wait," Justin called, jogging to catch up. "At least let me go with you."

"No, it's ok. I'm sure you have something better to do."

He put a hand over his heart, "Please, I insist. I wouldn't feel right allowing such a beautiful lady as yourself without some kind of protection. There are monsters in this world."

You would know. Elsa smiled, "Thank you, you're so kind." She walked on with Justin by her side. She was a bag of nerves having such a vicious killer right beside her. The fact that he had been hunting her down to kill her was even more nerve racking. She couldn't wait to reach the waterfall already. It seemed like the distance had tripled. Elsa glanced at him, "I didn't get your name."

He flashed her a toothy grin and she shuddered. He extended his hand to her, "Justin."

Elsa smiled and reluctantly placed her hand in his, "I'm Elsa." A shiver ran down her spine with the physical contact. She felt physically ill. She quickly pulled her hand from his and smiled. "It's nice to meet you, Justin." He smiled and ran his gaze down her body. Did she just detect appreciation and hunger in his gaze? She had to be imagining thing. The man sent to kill her couldn't be attracted to her. She doubted the heartless killer was even capable of emotion.

The waterfall came into view. *Finally.* She thought they would never get there. She had just has the longest walk of her life. She breathed a sigh of relief, now they next phase of the plan could be carried out. This would all be over soon. Elsa stopped walking, she glanced at Justin. "This is it. This is the water fall my boyfriend bought me to. Isn't it beautiful?"

Justin turned to study her, ignoring the waterfall. "Yes, it sure it beautiful." He took a step closer to Elsa and she stiffened. She remained still so as not to give herself away. "It sure is such a pity though," he whispered.

Elsa swallowed hard and turned to look up at him, "What is?"

"It is a pity that beautiful things sometimes have to be destroyed."

Elsa took as step away from him in the pretence of touching a plant. "Whatever do you mean Justin?"

"I wish things could have been different Elsa."

"You are confusing me Justin. Are you alright?"

He threw her a weird look and sighed, "I don't know."

"What's wrong?" Elsa asked as he took steps toward the pond. She didn't want to give the signal yet, it was too soon. Justin hadn't yet revealed his intentions. She looked at him expectantly, waiting for him to answer.

He smiled and stepped toward her, reaching out to touch her hair. She held her breath willing herself to stand still. He crushed a few, strands between his fingers. "You have such beautiful hair Elsa." He inhaled deeply, "You smell good to."

Elsa gawked at him. Was he being serious right now? She thought he wanted to killer, not admire her. She gave him a confused look, her brows furrowing. "Uh, thank you."

He smiled sadly at her, "I'm conflicted Elsa."

She nearly rolled her eyes; she was getting annoyed with the way he kept calling her name. Why didn't he hurry and make a move already? *At this rate we'll be here all night.* "What has you so conflicted?"

"Oh, Elsa I was sent to do something bad. But I have been finding it so hard to do."

Spit it out already. "What do you have to do?"

He chuckled and ran a hand down her bruised cheek. "Did your boyfriend give you these bruises?"

"No." She glared at him. He knew damn well who gave her the bruises. "So aren't you going to tell me what it is you have to do?"

"Oh right. I was sent to kill you Elsa. But following you around for so long, I guess I have become quite smitten with you." He let out a laugh, "Isn't that a hoot? I'm sorry for pushing you overboard the ship by the way, I'm glad you survived."

Elsa's breathing quickened, "Why do you want to kill me?"

"Because I was ordered to," he hissed s he grabbed her arm. "But I like you Elsa and it has been driving me insane. So, I've been killing other people to take the edge off. I really don't mean to but the thing inside me gets so *enraged*, you know?"

Elsa soon realized that Justin was not only a killer; he was also a very mentally sick man. "So what are you going to do now Justin?"

He grabbed her to him and attempted to kiss her. She pushed at his chest with all her might and ran. "Charles!" In the blink of an eye a huge wolf jumped out of the water and pounced after Justin. He dove out of the way, ready to flee; but he was stopped by another wolf. The animal rose up on hind legs and stopped down on Justin's chest, pinning him to the ground.

Elsa watched in horror as Justin began to shift. The other wolf bought a huge paw down on Justin's head, knocking the man unconscious. She let out a breath. For a minute she thought they would have to kill him. But they were able neutralize him; now he could be handed over to the authorities. Elsa pulled the cell phone from her pocket. She checked the screen and smiled; she had recorded Justin's confession about killing all those people. They had done it. Elsa watched as the large grey wolf ran into the bushes. A few moments later Victor emerged fully dressed.

"Good job Elsa. I guess I will take this one here and stash him somewhere until morning."

"What if he wakes up and makes a run for it?" Elsa asked.

"He isn't going anywhere. The silver chains I have will hold him until I can hand him over to the police."

Elsa ran to Victor and hugged him tightly. Taken aback at the unexpected show of affection, his eyes widened. His arms hesitantly wrapped around her. He was not use to having someone show him warmth. "Thank you Victor," she whispered. She gave him kiss on the cheek. He blinked several times and nodded, a smile spreading across his face. She let him go and walked over to Justin. He lifted the man over his shoulders and took off at a great speed.

Elsa blinked in amazement. "Wow shifters are really fast," she muttered. "Cool." She turned to the huge brown wolf staring at her. She approached cautiously; it was her first time being so close to Charles in wolf form. There was the day when she had seen him change from wolf to his human form, but she wasn't this close and she had fainted right after. She smiled slightly at the memory. She had been absolutely terrified, but not this time.

She reached a hand up to touch his face, "Charles?" The wolf bowed his head and she smiled. She scratched his head, "You are so adorable," she teased. He growled and she let out a laugh. "I'm sorry, I couldn't help myself." The wolf stepped back and she watched in awe as he shifted. Charles stood naked before her within seconds. "Wow, I will never get use to that," she whispered. She threw herself into his arms. He caught her in mid air. "Well we did it. Justin has been taken care of."

He set her down, "You were amazing Elsa."

She preened, "I was wasn't I? I deserve an award for my performance, don't you think?"

He chuckled, "I've got your award right here, baby." He lowered his head and covered her mouth. The kiss quickly became heated, passion blazing up between them like flames. He lifted his head, "What do you say make love one more time at this waterfall?"

She drew his head back down to her in answer, capturing his lips once more. Charles pushed at her clothes, trying to get rid of them. She quickly helped, shrugging them off. She stepped out of her pants and wrapped herself around him. He stepped back and jumped into the pool of water without warning. Elsa yelped as her body hit the cold water. "It's freezing," she breathed. She wondered how he and Victor had waited so long in the ice cold water.

"I'll warm you up," he whispered, nibbling at her neck. He spun around with her in his arms, bracing her against a tall smooth stone. "Are you alright? Is it too hard?"

"No," she murmured. "Take me now Charles."

"As you wish," he growled. He plunged into her in a swift powerful motion and sighed in satisfaction. Being inside of her always felt like coming home after a long time away. He captured her lips and urged the open. She parted her lips to allow him entrance, his tongue dipped inside and swept around, exploring the soft warmness of her mouth. Elsa moaned when Charles pushed into her with increasing force. She held on to him, her breaths coming in short puffs, she closed her eyes, loving the feel of his body against hers and of him inside of her. She didn't think she could get enough of him. Charles clenched his jaw, feeling himself approaching his orgasm, he pounded into Elsa relentlessly; satisfied when she let out a soft cry and came apart in his arms. His muscled bunched as he emptied himself inside of her.

Charles rested his head against her shoulder, still supporting her weight. She soon began to shiver against him. "It's time to get you dry," he whispered. The climbed out of the pool and quickly dressed.

Elsa dreaded the walk back to the hotel, "I'm so tired from all the excitement of the evening."

He grinned at her, "Hop on to my back."

She looked at him as if he had lost her mind, "What? Why?"

"Just hop on, I'll show you."

"Well ok. You have to stoop down a bit though."

He lowered himself so she could jump on to his back. "Hold on tight." Before Elsa could comment Charles took off at full speed. Her shriek was lost in the night breeze as he whizzed through the foliage. Elsa clung to him, holding on for dear life. She closed her eyes as the wind caressed her face. He stopped just as the hotel came into view.

Elsa laughed, "Oh my, that was exhilarating," she breathed. "When can we do that again?"

"Anytime you want." Charles laughed with her, taking pleasure in her merriment. He took her hand led her inside the hotel. Elsa headed straight for the bathroom. She wanted to shower and fall into bed. She stood under the spray of warm water. Charles stood in the door way, watching Elsa as she stood under the shower with her eyes closed. He thought of how much danger she had been in tonight and shuddered involuntarily. Justin had actually put his filthy hands on her. The twisted bastard had become infatuated with Elsa. Charles had heard every word Justin said. He had struggled to hold on to his self control as he listened to Justin's and Elsa's conversation. It had take every thin in him not to jump out of the pool and snap the man's neck. A low growl rumbled in his chest. He still thought it was a bad idea to let Justin live, he had a bad feeling about the entire thing. But, Elsa and Victor were convinced it was a good idea to turn the man over to the police.

Elsa turned to step out of the shower and jumped. She clutched her chest, "You're always sneaking up on me." She frowned when she notices the serious expression on his face. "What is it?"

"I'm worried about Justin still being alive. I should have killed him; he's too dangerous to live."

She caught his face between her hands. "But, he will be in the hands of the police. Once they have someone to place the responsibility of the murders on, we get to leave."

"The murders still could have been pinned on him if was dead all the same."

Elsa sighed, "Just let go of it now, it's over." She kissed him and sauntered off, stopping to look over her shoulder. "Hurry up and come join me in bed."

Chapter Five

Charles woke up to cheering coming from outside. What was going on out there? He sat up abruptly, turning to look out the window. The sun was shining though the curtain with full intensity. It must be late morning. He ran a hand over his face; he had slept late this morning. That didn't usually happen. He hadn't realized how tired he was. He smiled to himself, Elsa had managed o wear him out last night. They had made love two more times after getting back to their room. She had transformed from an innocent virgin to an insatiable minx. He had no problem with that because he could get enough of her. He looked down to see if she was still asleep.

He frowned as panic rose up in him. Where was she? He hopped out of bed and checked the bathroom. She was nowhere to be found. He threw on his clothes and rushed outside. He stood on the front steps of the hotel and searched the crow for Elsa. He couldn't find her anywhere. Why would she leave and not tell him? "Charles! You're awake." To his relief he heard her voice. He whipped around to see her approaching him with Victor at her side. He sighed; at least she'd had sense enough to have Victor with her. But he was still angry.

"Elsa, where the hell were you?" He barked.

Elsa stopped walking abruptly, taken aback by his tone. She frowned, "I just came out to find Victor. I wanted to make sure all had gone as according to planned." She brightened, putting the sharp tone he had used with her aside and rushed to him, excitement in her voice, "And it did. The police has Justin in custody, and we can board the ship soon. Isn't that great?"

Charles glared at her, "You should have woken me up if you wanted to come outside. It was stupid of you to run off on your own," he growled.

Elsa tried to hold on to her temper, "I really don't appreciate the tone you are taking with me Charles."

"If you don't like it then maybe you should be more careful with you damn life."

Elsa snapped, she'd had enough of him talking to her that way. She pointed her finger at him, "You have no right to talk to me like that. If you apologize now, I will forget the whole thing."

Charles seethed, "Maybe you are the one who should apologize for being less than smart; running around on your own, without telling me."

"And who are you my boss? I don't have to report to you," she scoffed.

Victor cleared his throat, he felt uncomfortable butting into the lovers' quarrel, but they were attracting attention. "You two are garnering an audience." Both Elsa and Charles swung around to see a few people glancing their way.

Charles shifted his gaze back to Elsa, "Get inside; we can talk about this later."

"Still feel like you should give me orders do you? Well, I'm not going anywhere with you," she hissed. She turned and stomped down the steps.

"Elsa get back here." She pretended not to hear him and kept walking until she was lost in the crowd. She was furious. How dare he talk to her like that? All she had done was leave the room for a little while. Was that such a crime? She couldn't understand why he was so upset. Elsa decided to find Tabitha and Arnold to lighten her mood. It didn't take long for her to locate them; they were in their usual spot.

She smiled brightly, "Hi you two. Are you as excited as I am about the news?"

Tabitha beamed, "Oh we are absolutely delighted. It's about time they found that rotten man. Can you believe he worked on the ship?" She shuddered, "I thing he even carried my bags to our cabin. He was actually in out cabin, I could just faint at the knowledge."

"He looked like such a nice young man. It only goes to show how deceiving looks can be," Arnold muttered.

Elsa nodded, " I am glad he is right where he belong."

Tabitha shuddered "Did you hear that he will be travelling back to Miami with us? Can you imagine? We will have to spend a few more days with that man on the ship *again*."

Elsa looked at Tabitha in horror. She had no idea that Justin would be travelling back with them. She hadn't even thought that was a possibility. A cold feeling settled inside her stomach. Maybe Charles had been right; perhaps the best thing to do was really to kill Just. She thought of how easy it would for the shifter to escape on the ship and begin wreaking havoc once again. She visibly paled; he would come after her with a vengeance. She had after all played a major part in his capture; deliberately leading him out into the woods. All of a sudden she felt extra vulnerable. She wanted to rush back to Charles and burrow herself into his arms and hide from the world. That is where she knew she would feel safe.

"Are you alright dear? You look so pale," Tabitha observed.

Elsa nodded, before she could respond, everyone's attention was shifted to the man standing on the front steps of the hotel, demanding everyone's attention. "Good morning ladies and gentlemen, can I have your attention please. You all might have heard by now that the man behind the vicious killings has been apprehended. We have the man in custody, so you can all begin boarding the ship as early as possible tomorrow morning." A cheer erupted from the crowd.

"It's about time!" Someone shouted.

"I want s refund!" Another man shouted, "This was the worst vacation I have ever been on." Multiple members of the crowd agreed loudly.

Elsa could care less about the money but she was in full agreement with the part about this being the worst vacation ever. The luxurious Caribbean cruise had turned out to be a nightmare of blood and death.

Not to mention dark secrets about her life. She blew out a breath, on the bright side; she had fallen madly in love. Of course she was upset with the man she had fallen in love with, but that was beside the point. The way she felt about him had not changed and she doubted it ever would. She almost turned to make her way through the crow to fin Charles, but her pride won. She refused to speak to him until he apologized for the way he had spoken to her.

Elsa opened the door to the hotel room. She pushed her head inside and glanced around. The room was empty; Charles was nowhere to be seen. Her heart fell slightly in disappointment. She had spent the rest of the day with Arnold and Tabitha exploring and hanging out by the beach. She had deliberately avoided coming back to the room until it was dark. She had left the older couple to come back to the room to get her things together. She wanted to be on that ship the first chance she got in the morning. She had expected Charles to be here waiting. She hadn't seen him all day. She stepped inside with a sigh and closed the door. May be he was still upset with her from their argument. She busied herself packing. She would just wait in the room until he got back; he would have to return at some point during the night. As soon as he walked through the door, Elsa decided that she was going to tell him that she loved him. She could no longer keep it to herself; he had to know. She sighed, whether he felt the same way for her not, her feelings would be made known.

Elsa jumped when she heard a loud crash sound. What was that? She couldn't place exactly where the sound had come from. She heard a scream a few minutes later. Her heart thudded in her chest and she groaned out loud. What was it this time? She rushed to the door and pulled it open to investigate. She walked down the hallway and saw nothing. Maybe the sound had come from downstairs. She head for the staircase. As soon as she turned the corner, she saw a crowd forming at a doorway. She heard gasps and murmurs. "It's happening all over again," she heard someone whispered.

"The killer has escaped!"

"Or maybe there is more than one killer."

Elsa listened to the comments as she approached. A shiver ran down her spine. Why were they still talking about the killer? She was almost afraid to see what took place in the room. She swallowed and forced herself to peer into the hotel room. It was painted with blood; she stepped forward to see two bodies lying on the floor. Her heart stopped when she saw Tabitha staring up at her blankly. *No, no. It can't be.* It was Tabitha and Arnold. A strangled sound escaped her lip. Her breathing became fast and shallow. A fine sheen of cold sweat washed her skin; the grief and disbelief inside of her threatened to cut off her breath. She backed away from the room and the sight of all that blood. It was Justin, she knew it was. He had somehow escaped and was out for revenge. He had come after Tabitha and Arnold, know that she held them dear. She shook her head, trying to get rid of the image of her friends' torn and ravaged bodies.

She began to shiver uncontrollably. The walls closed in around her and the room started to darken. *Oh no.* She was going to faint. She swayed, trying to fight off the feeling. Her knees buckled and she the floor rushed up to meet her. Charles swept her up before she hit the floor, "I've got," he whispered. The darkness engulfed her completely.

Charles strode quickly down the hallway with Elsa in his arms. He glanced down at her. She was deathly pale. He had been out in the woods still brooding over their argument earlier. He had decided to leave Elsa alone for the remainder of the day until she cooled off. He had been padding in the foliage in his wolf form not too far from the hotel, but far enough to avoid being seen. He had heard the commotion with his enhanced hearing and immediately shifted back to his human form to come and investigate. He had run in to Victor who was running to do just the same. Victor had glance at him, his expression trouble, "Its Justin."

Charles had nodded, "I know I can smell him all over the place. The bastard has escaped."

Victor ran a hand through his hair, "We have to find Elsa now. He's going to go after her." But Victor had been wrong; Justin had not gone after Elsa. He had targeted her friends. Charles had smelled Tabitha's and Arnold's blood before he rounded the corner. His stomach had churned, he knew they were dead. Sadness had washed over him; he had become fond of the older couple because the care so much for Elsa. She would be torn apart by their deaths. He had to keep her away from the scene. But he had been too late; he had approached the crow to see Elsa staring in horror at the gruesome scene. When he saw her sway, he had rushed forward to catch her before she hit the ground.

Victor met him at the staircase. He stared wide eyed at a lifeless and pale Elsa lying limply in Charles's arms. "My God, what happened? Is she alright?"

"She fainted; she's a bit squeamish when it comes to blood."

Victor glanced at her pallor, "*Just* a bit?"

Charles glanced at Victor, "I can't take her back to our room; there is a good chance Justin knows where it is. He could be there waiting as we speak."

"Take her to my room." Charles followed Victor to a far end of the large building. He pushed open the door and stepped aside so Charles could enter.

"We have to find Justin and kill him now," Charles said, placing Elsa on a long sofa. "He is more dangerous than ever; he's angry."

"*Damn it.* Charles, you were right, we should have killed the bastard when we had the chance."

Elsa stirred on the couch; bring both men's attention to her. She moaned softly and her eyes fluttered open. Her eyes swept over her surroundings in confusion. Where was she? How did she get here? Charles rushed to her side. "Charles, I'm so sorry I walked away earlier," she rushed out groggily. Her mind was fuzzy, but she remembered their argument this morning.

"It's alright, that's not important."

"Where am I? What happened?"

"This is Victor's room."

She looked around; spotting Victor, she smiled weakly at him. What was she doing in Victor's room? She paused; *I fainted again*, she thought, annoyed with herself. In that moment, everything came rushing back to her. She bolted upward as her memories flooded back. Her breath hitched in her throat. *Tabitha and Arnold;* they were dead. Her eyes flew to Charles; his grave expression confirmed it. He looked away from her. Elsa let out a keening cry, the sound coming up from the bottom of her belly. "*No.*" She hugged her self and rocked back and forth. "I killed them," she uttered, the words barely audible.

Charles tuned her to face him with his finger tips, "Do say that Elsa. Justin did this."

"Because of me," she whispered. The tears streamed down her face and she stared ahead, unseeing.

Charles sighed and stood up. Elsa was gone; he mind was nowhere near here. He glanced at her, concerned; as he stared into space. He turned to Victor, "You stay here with her. I'm going to find Justin."

Victor shook his head, "No, let me go. The man is dangerous and strong; an he's out for blood. If I don't come back its fine," he glanced at Elsa. "But she needs you, if anything happens to you... I don't think she would be able to manage losing you too, Charles."

Charles stared at Victor intently. "I'm going, but I will come back." There was deadly conviction in his voice. He intended to make Justin pay for causing Elsa so much pain. He was going to remove the threat to her once and for all. The beast rippled inside of him anticipating the fight and the taste of Justin's blood. Charles's eyes flashed a bright yellow. "I'm going to rip his heart out," he growled.

Victor blinked, somewhat surprised at what he saw in Charles's eyes. Even he was a bit afraid of the man in that moment. He nodded, "Very well Charles, make sure you remove him from this world forever."

"Charles no," Elsa's soft voice sounded behind them. Charles whipped around to look at her; the deadly purpose in his eyes was quickly replaced by tenderness. She got up and walked to him. "Don't go; I don't want to get hurt."

"I have to this Elsa. I have to get rid of him once and for all; for your safety and for everyone else on this island."

"But what if you don't come back? I need you to come back," she sniffed. "I love you Charles."

He stared down at her, wondering if he had heard her correctly. She loved him. Joy blossomed across his heart like a field of flowers in springtime. He let out a breath. "I love you too, Elsa." Her breath hitched and she wrapped her arms around him. He held her tightly. The happiness he felt in that moment knew no bounds; the woman he so desperately loved had just expressed her love for him. Now more than ever, he was determined to live. "I will come back to you Elsa," he promised. He now had something else to fight for; he would fight for love. He would fight for a chance of a happy life with Elsa.

She pulled back to look at him, "I'm going with you."

He blanched, "Like hell you are. You're staying right here until I get back."

"But I-

He planted a hard kiss on her lips, moving his mouth over hers with a new intensity, fuel by love. She kissed him back with everything she had. When he finally pulled away, she felt bereft. He repeated, "You're staying right here." He turned and to Victor, who gave him a nodded. He opened the door and disappeared.

Elsa stared after him, with her heart in her mouth. She prayed that he came back to her. She couldn't imagine her life without him. She would be lost without Charles.

Charles took off into the dark woods, shedding his clothes as he moved. His bones elongated as he shifted into his wolf form. The night was dark but he could see clearly as if it was day. He smelled Justin; he was nearby. He knew he was waiting for him. He spotted the black wolf and let out a growl.

Justin chuckled inside of his wolf. *Charles, we meet again. Tell me, did Elsa like the gifts I left her?*

Charles sneered; *you will pay for that Justin, with your life.*

Justin shook his head. *I thought about killing her as soon as I escaped. But, I thought it would be more fun to watch her suffer a bit. She must be devastated about her to old friends.* He let out a laugh. *I will kill her right after I kill you.*

Charles crouched low; ready for Justin to attack. Justin got right to it. He roared and took off, sharp fangs bared. Charles waited until the other wolf was nearly upon him before he swerved out of his path. Just in landed, his paws making a loud thud; before he could turn to make another attack, Charles jumped on his back; clamping his teeth around his neck. He bit down hard, savoring the gush of blood that prayed into his mouth. Justin tried to shake him off, but he maintained his deathly grip. He gave one final snap. The cracking of bones was deafening in the night. Justin went limp and his body shrank, returning to human form.

Charles knew he had to behead the other shifter or remove his heart to kill him. He shifted and knelt beside Justin's still body. His claws remained extended. He pushed into Justin's chest cavity with crushing force and pulled back, taking the pulsating organ with him. He threw it into the distance and stood up, looking down at the dead man with disgust. This was the fate he deserved for taking so many innocent lives and for his crimes against Elsa.

Elsa paced the floor of Victor's room. She bit her nails and occasionally ran her fingers through her hair in agitation. What was taking Charles so long? What if he was hurt or worse? Her mind raced with the many possibilities of what could have happened. She closed her eyes; she should have gone with him. He never should have gone alone. She resumed her pacing. "For goodness sake Elsa, you're about to wear holes in the floor. Sit down, will you? You're making me nervous," Victor stated.

"We should go and look for him, Victor."

"He is fine. He can hold his own; I've seen that for myself on several occasions. He will come back soon."

"But why is he taking so long? What if he's lay hurt somewhere?"

"Charles is fine."

Elsa growled, she was on the verge of tearing out her hair. She has never been so edge in her life. Victor shook his head when she started to pace again. He hoped Charles came back soon, before Elsa lost her mind.

A knock sounded on the door. Elsa dashed to open it. Victor stepped in front of her, "You stay back." He walked to the door, "Who is there?"

"Open the bloody door Victor, it's me," Charles roared.

Victor opened the door and grinned at the sight of Charles, "Glad to see you are still in one piece my friend." He stepped aside to allow Charles inside.

"*Charles*," Elsa breathed. She was relieved beyond belief. She flew in to his arms, with such force; he stubble backward, but steadied himself. She pulled back to study hi, "Are you ok? Are you hurt?"

He grinned, "I'm fine."

Her shoulders sagged in relief. "I was so worried you wouldn't come back to me."

"I'm here, my love."

She smiled up at him, her eyes shining with tears.

Chapter Six

Elsa stood on the balcony outside of Charles's cabin. She stared into the distance as the ship sailed through the sea. A light breeze whipped her auburn tresses around her face. Her dress fluttered around her in the wind. They were finally heading back to Miami. The ship had left the port of Great Harbor Cay that morning. Everyone had been ecstatic; anxious to leave behind the horrors of their blood stained vacation. Justin's body had been discovered. The police had been puzzled over how he had managed to escape. They had been even more puzzled by his mysterious death. But, everyone had rejoiced, knowing that the monster was gone for good.

Elsa though of everything Justin had done to her; everything he had taken from her. The tears ran down her cheeks at the memory of Tabitha and Arnold. She had grown to love the older couple so much; and Justin had so callously taken their lives. She sniffed; it was losing a second set of parents. But she was not so lonely this time around. She now had Charles and Victor. She smiled when she remembered her friend in Georgia; she also had Lisa; who would be livid when she found out why she had not heard from Elsa in so long. *Boy will I have some stories to tell Lisa.* She knew she had to keep certain details a secret; after all she couldn't let Lisa in on the secret that her boyfriend was a shape shifter when she introduced them.

She let out a breath. Her life had been changed forever. She now knew the true cause of her parents' death and that she had the wolf shifter gene. She and Charles had discussed the possibility of him converting her to full wolf shifter in the future. She wasn't ready for that quite yet; but she knew deep down that she would eventually want to do it. She would do anything to be with her life mate forever. She had been elated when Charles had expressed that he wanted them to start a life together. She had no problem moving to England and he had no reservations about staying in the United States. She smiled; they had agreed that they would go back and forth between both countries. That way, she would get to see Victor in England often. So, she was not going to return to her dull, lonely life after all.

She heard the door slide open behind her. Charles stepped out onto the balcony. "You've been crying."

She sighed, "I was just thinking of Arnold and Tabitha." Her bottom lip trembled when she called their names. She bit down to keep herself from bursting into tears.

He wiped away her tears with his thumbs, "I'm so sorry Elsa." He pulled her into his embrace. "I have something that might cheer you up." He pulled his cell phone out of his pocket and handed it to her.

She took it, throwing him a confused look. She looked down at the phone and her eyes widened. There were twenty-five missed calls from Lisa's number. "She's going to kill me," Elsa groaned. No doubt Lisa had been worried when she didn't hear from Elsa. She had promised to keep in contact after all.

Charles grinned, "I'm sure she will forgive you when you tell her you were grounded on an island with a killer on the loose."

Elsa giggled, "She will forgive me alright, and she will probably be scared to take vacations for the rest of her life." She looked down at the phone, "I should call her."

"Go right ahead, I'll be inside." He gave her a kiss on the forehead and went back inside. She quickly dialled Lisa's number.

"Hello?"

"Hi, Lisa."

"Oh my God, Elsa. What happened to you? I called a million times trying to find out if you were ok. I didn't get any e-mails or phone calls for days. I was sick with worry. I was ready to call in the coast guards for Christ's sake."

"Lisa slow down. Take a breath."

She heard her friend take several breaths, "Ok, I'm good. Are you alright?"

"I am now. The ship had to make an emergency stop on an island and I had no way of communicating with you. The phone was left on the ship and we weren't allowed back on until a few murder investigations were through."

Lisa gasped, "Oh my. I told you to have fun honey; but that sounds like way too much excitement."

Elsa giggled, "Tell me about it. Anyway we will reach Miami soon and I'll be home in no time. I will tell you everything; and you will get to meet my boyfriend."

"*Oh*. Boyfriend huh? Is it the hot English guy, Charles?"

"Yes, he's the one."

Lisa gave a loud shriek, "Hurry up and get here girl! I can't wait. I'm so glad you're ok."

"Thanks Lisa. I'll see you soon."

"Bye honey."

Elsa hung up the phone, smiling from ear to ear. She missed Lisa's overly excited and dramatic responses to everything. She couldn't wait to sit down with her friend and talk about everything, especially Charles. She wanted to share her happiness. She walked into the Cabin to find Charles.

"So has Lisa forgiven all?" He asked.

"She's just glad I'm alright. I can't wait for you to meet her; she is just so much fun. Her personality will blow you away."

Charles laughed, "I can't wait. Come here."

She sauntered over to where he sat on the sofa. He patted his lap and she sat down. He looked up at her, "We finally get to home and have a little peace."

Elsa frowned, "Don't forget that there are still a few wolf shifters out there who wants me dead."

Fierce determination flashed in Charles's eyes, "They won't ever touch you Elsa. I will kill everyone who even looks at you in the wrong way."

She shivered when his eyes flashed yellow, revealing a glimpse of the wolf inside him. She knew she would always be safe with him. He shifted so that she was lying beneath him. He placed her hand above her head and kissed her deeply. Desire clouded her eyes when she gazed up at him. He ginned as he began slowly to undress her; holding her gaze. She smiled back him seductively. He leaned down to flutter soft kisses over her face, then fining her lips again. His had caressed her body, causing her to moan and arched her body closer to his. He moved to trailed kisses down neck. Her breathing soon quickened.

"I love you Elsa. Promise you will stay with me forever."

"I will Charles, forever. I love you too, with all of my heart."

Love gleamed in his eyes before he leaned down to capture her lips.

Don't miss out!

Visit the website below and you can sign up to receive emails whenever Alice Jamison publishes a new book. There's no charge and no obligation.

https://books2read.com/r/B-A-VMLC-HAPQ

BOOKS2READ

Connecting independent readers to independent writers.

Did you love *Deadly Secrets Box Set Volumes 1 - 3 Billionaire Shape-Shifter Romance Series*? Then you should read *Deadly Secrets Free (Billionaire Shape-Shifter Romance Series Book 4)*[1] by Alice Jamison!

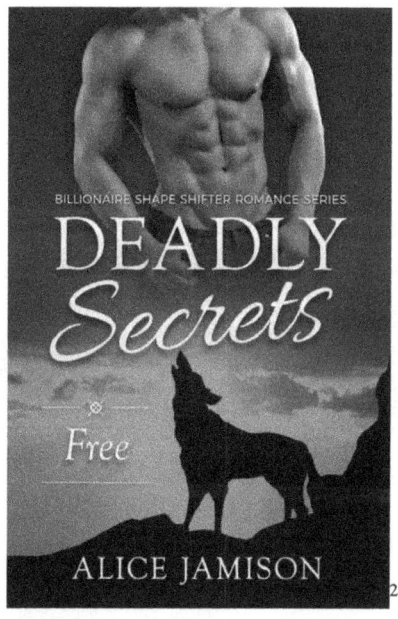

After making dark and deadly discoveries and narrowly escaping death Elsa Grey finally has everything she has ever wanted but thought she would never have. She has found a man that she loves and wants to spend the rest of her life with and she has made a discovery that will change her life forever. Happiness is finally within reach. But, there is one problem. Everything can be snatched away from her at anytime. With danger still lurking around the corner, she lives in fear of losing everything. She wants nothing but to be free. Charles Grimm's lonely existence has been replaced by happiness and love. He has fought hard

---

1. https://books2read.com/u/baplGx

2. https://books2read.com/u/baplGx

to hold on to the cause for his happiness, but deadly enemies still threaten to take her away. He will stop at nothing to protect the woman he loves. Will he be able to free them both from the peril that hinders true happiness or will he end up losing everything that he holds dear?

Also by Alice Jamison

Agony, Ecstasy & Crime
Agony, Ecstasy & Crime Fatal Vows
Agony, Ecstasy & Crime You Are My Drug
Agony, Ecstasy & Crime Disappeared Book 3

Bloodlust
Bloodlust Disturbing the Peace
Bloodlust A New Thirst Book

Cool Blue
Cool Blue After Midnight A Bad Boy Romance
Cool Blue Molten Gold A Bad Boy Romance
Cool Blue Passion Red A Bad Boy Romance
Cool Blue Midnight Black A Bad Boy Romance

Deadly Secrets
Deadly Secrets The Shadow (Billionaire Shape-Shifter Romance Series Book 1)

Deadly Secrets Secrets Revealed (Billionaire Shape-Shifter Romance Series Book 2)
Deadly Secrets The Fight for Love (Billionaire Shape-Shifter Romance Series Book 3)
Deadly Secrets Free (Billionaire Shape-Shifter Romance Series Book 4)
Deadly Secrets Threats (Billionaire Shape-Shifter Romance Series Book 5)
Deadly Secrets Torn Apart (Billionaire Shape-Shifter Romance Series Book 6
Deadly Secrets Escape (Billionaire Shape-Shifter Romance Series Book 7)
Deadly Secrets Peace (Billionaire Shape-Shifter Romance Series Book 8)

Enchanted Souls Series
Enchanted Souls Series Moonlight
Enchanted Souls Series Tour book 2
Enchanted Souls Series The Secret Of The Glow Book 3
Enchanted Souls Series Return To Crested Valley Book 4
Enchanted Souls Series Forever Book 5

Passion Lust And Fire
Passion Lust And Fire Claim Me Like There's No Tomorrow Book 1
If I Can't Have You No One Can
Passion Lust And Fire Whispers Of The Night Book 3

Seducing The Billionaire

Seducing The Billionaire The Barista And The Billionaire Book 1
A Prince's Betrayal The Barista And The Billionaire Book 2
Chaos of Past Secrets The Barista And The Billionaire Book 3
Engaged in a Whirlwind Weekend The Barista And The Billionaire Book 4
The Final Encounter The Barista And The Billionaire

The Penthouse
The Penthouse (The Meeting Part Two)
The Penthouse (The Rules Part Three)
The Penthouse The Offer Part Four
The Penthouse Part One

Wolf Quest
Wolf Quest: Temptation of the Wolf
Wolf Quest: Passion Of The Wolf Book 2
Wolf Quest: Pleasure Of The Wolf Book 3

World's End
World's End Apocalypse Drake Book 1
World's End: Artificial Drake Book 2
World's End: Wings Of Drake Book 3

Standalone
Vampire Magic
Her Secret Tiger

Deadly Secrets Box Set Volumes 1 - 3 Billionaire Shape-Shifter Romance Series
Enchanted Souls Series Bundle (Books 1 - 3)
Gentle Push
Kill Me Gently With Passion
Cool Blue A Bad Boy Romance 1 - 4 Bundle
Gentle Push, Her Secret Tiger, Kill Me Gently With Passion 3 Book Bundle
World's End 3 Book Bundle
Mithir and Verona The Dragon's Surrender
A Secret Shade Of Mysterious Bear Shifters
This World Is Full Of Men
He's Watching Me
I'll Always Have Your Back (A Bad Boy Billionaire Romance)
A Mysterious Bad Boy
Spice
I Thought You Were the One
Get out of my Life
The Penthouse The Call Part 5
Wolf Quest: 3 Book Bundle
A Billionaire Romance Series Bundle Books 1 - 5 The Penthouse
7 Erotica Bundle Stories Hot Stories Of Sex, BDSM, Domination And Submission That Will Make You Wet!

CPSIA information can be obtained
at www.ICGtesting.com
Printed in the USA
LVHW110814230422
717039LV00021B/531